Shlomo Kalo / THRILLER

Do not come praising friendship to me

Do not come praising harmony

Come praising independence

Praise human dignity

Original Hebrew title: *THRILLER*

English translation by Philip Simpson

© All Rights Reserved
Y   D.A.T. Publications
POBox 27019,
Jaffa 61270, Israel
www.y-dat.com
dat@y-dat.co.il
ISBN: 978-965-7028-62-9

Cover: The author and his wife

Cover design: Akira007 / akiragrficz

To Rivka, my wife

I salute you

Shlomo Kalo

THRILLER*

The Galilee Plot

---

* Fiction, the product of creative imagination, for the
diversion and entertainment, in times of leisure or
insomnia, of reader and author alike.

Table of Contents

CHAPTER ONE... 9

CHAPTER TWO... 17

CHAPTER THREE...................................... 20

CHAPTER FOUR... 27

CHAPTER FIVE... 45

CHAPTER SIX... 48

CHAPTER SEVEN...................................... 53

CHAPTER EIGHT....................................... 55

CHAPTER NINE... 64

CHAPTER TEN... 68

CHAPTER ELEVEN.................................... 74

CHAPTER TWELVE................................... 83

CHAPTER THIRTEEN.............................. 93

CHAPTER FOURTEEN............................. 103

CHAPTER FIFTEEN.................................. 107

CHAPTER SIXTEEN................................. 113

CHAPTER SEVENTEEN......................... 120

CHAPTER EIGHTEEN............................. 134

CHAPTER NINETEEN............................. 145

CHAPTER TWENTY................................. 164

CHAPTER TWENTY-ONE..................... 182

EPILOGUE.. 188

APPENDIX A... 192

APPENDIX B... 196

The author and his works........ 198

CHAPTER ONE

It was a particularly pleasant summer this year – a summer which was to degenerate into anger and upheavals, and natural disasters – and as every year, I spent it with my wife in a quiet and comfortable hotel, well known and not inexpensive, in Switzerland. In the very same room in which my recent books have been written, including this one. For the benefit of patrons not conversant with German, the management of the hotel provided an English newspaper, the "Herald Tribune" which we read avidly, even rising early to be sure of seeing it. The number of copies was limited, and the first into the dining room in the morning would get the paper.

We sat beside the teapots and the bowls of cereal. My wife was leafing through the paper. Suddenly she stopped leafing as her eyes focussed on something, presumably important and relevant, so I supposed, to our home country. And my supposition proved to be correct, as she handed the paper to me, pointing to an item on the front page, in the lower left-hand corner. A short item headlined: *Mystery disease erupts in the mixed village of Hasda, in Galilee.* I read the article, or more precisely, I devoured every word, every letter. The paper reported that Hasda, the only settlement of its kind, with Jewish and Arab families living side by side, founded not long ago with the aid of a generous grant from the Saudis, had been struck by a mysterious and as yet undiagnosed disease: symptoms included high temperature, prolonged and debilitating fever – but it was definitely not any form of malaria. Some twenty families had been affected, half of them Jewish and half of them Arab. Within two weeks, ten patients had died. And the astonishing thing – the paper reported with no small degree of smug satisfaction, proud of the achievement of its intrepid correspondent, in finding the story had an "astonishing" element – was that all ten were, without exception, Jews and Jews exclusively.

Two young families of Jewish idealists, who came to break down the barriers of hatred, fear and prejudice, had perished, parents and children alike. The authorities were investigating. As previously noted, the disease itself was yet to be diagnosed.

"Do you remember that story of yours," my

wife asked me, "about some way of infecting only Jews with some virus or other? There was a young Arab – you studied together, or rather you did your postgraduate studies together in the U.S.A – and he came up with this crazy idea, and you tried to convince me that in principle it was possible..."

I smiled a forced smile.

"It looks as if he's done it," I replied, rereading the succinct report in the prestigious journal and in the process asking myself repeatedly – had the thing really been done, taken out of the realm of theory and laboratory exploration, and put into practice, on the ground?

Amin Abu Halil I had met at Columbia University, a distinguished institution of higher education with a worldwide reputation, especially for its faculty of natural sciences. We were both up for the degree of Ph.D.; he got his and I remained an M.Sc. I wasn't too disappointed. The whole Ph.D. thing had a hefty portion of snobbery about it, without the slightest trace of sincerity or any interest in genuine research – all the excuses and justifications of those infected by banal-intellectualist laziness. I expressed my opinion to Amin; despite the tradition of mutual hostility that had grown up and still existed in our disputed homeland, or perhaps because of it, we often talked and relations between us were decidedly friendly. He didn't accept my opinion, nor did he reject it out of hand. He justified his studies by reminding me he had been sent here at the expense of some Arab educational fund, and he had absolutely no intention of disappointing his sponsors, especially since the administrators of the fund, it transpired, expected great and glorious things of him. Amin proved himself and was duly awarded his Ph.D. for a thesis focussing in particular on Rickettsias, as distinct from my more modest endeavours, studying the micro-organisms responsible for plagues and in particular P.Pestis which created havoc, so it seems, in the Middle Ages, with a number of outbreaks in the world of the developing nations, not correctly diagnosed as such. I often talked with Amin about our research and about other subjects. Our conversations were characterised by open-heartedness and flawless sincerity.

He did not hide his opinion that the greatest plague of humanity, casting down into Hell its pride and all its noble aspirations, is caused by no micro-organism but rather by a parasitical macro-organism, walking on two legs, belonging to the restricted and exclusive and loathsome strain of the Jewish community, whose much vaunted culture is decidedly anti-cultural. National chauvinism, unbridled pursuit of profit, arrogance and cunning, arousing in the most direct, simple and natural way, murderous hatred to say the least, and more precisely – aversion. And all the nations that call themselves enlightened, have cast them out from within their borders and installed them in the desert, on the understanding that there they enjoy, according to the ancient writings, certain rights. And this "desert", as it turned out, had been inhabited since time immemorial by "fools", law-abiding people and respecters of tradition, whose hard lives allow no parasitical creatures to share the desert with them. Here he would preach an impassioned sermon about attempts to tackle this morbid evil, Jews and Judaism, starting with the Roman Empire, through the Middle Ages, the statement of Erasmus: "If it is a Christian virtue to hate the Jews, then we are all good Christians", the Nazis in the more recent past and the Arabs today. The debate was heated and like any debate, it was futile from its foundations to its lofty pinnacles. I brought up all the atrocities committed by the Roman Empire, the dark days of the Middle Ages, the Hell of Nazi ideology, and the devilish, magnified reflection of these three elements in the present day, in Arab terrorism, the heroes of which are methodical murderers, devoid of conscience and devoid of heart, whose sole aspiration is murder for murder's sake. In spite of this, we continued to hold conversations, only in English, naturally enough. Amin resolutely refused even to curse in Hebrew. Amin Abu Halil knew the language perfectly well, and his Hebrew was as fluent as mine, but he insisted he had sworn a vow not to speak it, read it or write it, since it was the language of the conqueror of his land and the oppressor of his people. I was not bothered either way, so we spoke in English, the language which we shared, and it may be that in the course of our intense efforts to express ourselves to each other, the standard of our spoken English improved, something we could both be grateful for.

The great and the glorious times of the Arabs, Amin Abu Halil was not well informed about, and when the gaps in his knowledge were shown to him, the result was helpless fury. He was particularly enraged when I pointed out to him that during the eighteenth and early nineteenth centuries, the principal livelihood of the western "Maghrebi" Arabs, the inhabitants, that is, of present-day Libya, Morocco, Tunisia and Algeria, was based on prostitution and piracy. I even found a dubious point of light on this dark page of Arab history, when America, a young country in those days, negotiated with the above-mentioned nations and offered a generous ransom, on condition that ships flying the American flag would not be attacked by Arab pirates, and the agreement was made and implemented...

Amin Abu Halil smiled and then burst into loud laughter, making his whole body shake:

"My ancestors," he said emphatically, "did something for the good of humanity, removing the democratic mask from the faces of those devoid of honour and faith. And what about the Europeans?" he asked – "Weren't they included in the agreement? After all, they are no less female than those Americans, in fact they are their legal and illegal ancestors; you can be sure that among those who came up with the idea and did the negotiating, there were a fair number of Jews..."

"That's possible," I answered him, "I don't know the details. As far as Europe is concerned, Britain and France took on the pirates and beat them."

"The Arabs have a mission", he declared in a tone of firm conviction.

"And that is?"

"To cleanse the world from spiritual whoredom and I'm talking about the so-called 'progressive' American-European nations, which are polluting the holy land of God."

I offered him a ceasefire: "Did you know, you're quoting Osama Bin Laden?"

"That was my intention," he explained and added: "And what, in your opinion, should be suggested to these cultural nations, that call themselves 'progressive'...

It seemed that a ceasefire was in force. I

clung to it:

"To stop polluting the holy land of God."

"Your answers are typically Jewish."

"And what do you suggest?"

"To accept what you say."

"Accept the answer of a Jew?"

"Accept it and implement it!" my interlocutor declared, with an enthusiasm that could not be described as other than quintessentially Mediterranean, based, if it has a base, on impulsiveness, which beyond any shadow of a doubt is not to be trusted at all, like any form of impulsiveness.

And this was clear to both of us. The question remained to be answered, how to make progress in this impulsive Middle East, so that it may learn something from something, from what is the opposite of impulsiveness.

"The only true and accurate answer is: it's impossible to achieve this."

"We shall all know before too long," he commented simply.

On this there was full agreement – Mediterranean agreement.

CHAPTER TWO

We studied with the same professor – one of the greatest luminaries of human microbiology, Mick Antonio, born in Canada, from emphatically British roots. His affection for the pair of us was obvious for all to see, and aroused some envy. Despite this, he didn't invite us to dine at his house, unlike his other pupils, who were neither Jews nor Arabs, although we were both reckoned the elite among his students, and we not only earned praise from him, but quite often, if a student was falling behind he would be referred to us for some extra coaching.

After Amin was awarded his doctorate, and I voluntarily excluded myself from the ranks of doctoral candidates, the professor talked with us in his office, separately. I was the first to be invited. The esteemed professor launched immediately into a tirade: "Why do you people tolerate those beasts of the desert among you, you who are the bearers of the flag of human culture and progress, and have been so since time immemorial? All the western nations revere those who have emerged from your midst – Jesus Christ and Karl Marx. You come up with advice about everything and without you, the practical use of the atom would never have come to fruition. Finish them off! I respect your refusal to go for the degree of Ph.D., along with that character, El-Husseini," – he corrupted Amin's name and continued without embarrassment – "or Abdul el-Said, or whatever his name is, who cares, impossible to pronounce anyway. So please do something! Liberate humanity from these murderous monsters!"

After me, Amin Abu Halil went in and received a lecture in the same spirit, although not identical. "Why are you people proclaiming Jihad? Do it, don't just proclaim it! Liberate the world from those leeches, put an end to the 'Elders of Zion'! Talking of honour and culture and progress and standing helpless before a gang of leeches! Finish them off, crush them. Bring about their definitive end, once and for all, and earn the gratitude of all the great nations, nations of honour and culture, in the past, present and future. Enough of speeches and demonstrations. One of your greatest men demanded that every Arab should kill a Jew. If every self-respecting Arab can kill two – what's wrong with that! Do something, so you'll have a part in building the new world. So you'll be its princes! You have the oil, soak all the Jews in a sea of oil and set them alight."

We met after the personal meetings with the esteemed professor, and told one another what had happened there.

"What do you think?" asked Amin, with deep sadness reflected in his habitually gloomy eyes.

"You're asking for my opinion, the opinion of a Jew?" I pressed him.

"Yes. In the situation we're faced with, there's no one else to ask."

"I'll tell you my impressions, which are decidedly objective impressions. The esteemed professor is inciting us against one another. He wants to get rid of us both, at a stroke, and he's leaving the job to us."

"What's to be done?"

"An unnecessary question. You know as well as I do what has to be done."

"All the same," he asked again, "what's to be done?"

"What logic requires."

"What does logic require?" Amin persisted.

"Not to obey it. And the rest follows."

"To do the opposite!" Amin declared.

"Explicitly!" I stressed.

CHAPTER THREE

Several months passed. The two of us continued to hang around the university, with its lofty marble halls, pleasantly cool in the summer, comfortably warm in the winter, its massive libraries, its sophisticated laboratories, friendly locals. Amin's bursary did not end – on the contrary, for reasons best known to the sponsors, it was doubled.

My own, personal resources, I usually managed to avoid wasting in their entirety.

We did a lot of revelling, the kind of revelry appropriate to our age. We didn't come across any craze that we didn't dabble in. We found girlfriends of dubious character. Those that Amin chose were more glamorous, laden with strident jewellery. The ones who came out with me had no glamour about them at all, and it seemed they weren't even interested in such things. I drank. Amin refused to be my partner in sin.

His religion apparently prohibits this – so

he told me.

"And what about drugs?" I asked a pertinent question.

"We're not talking about them."

"Well?" I pressed him.

"Everyone can do as he pleases." He was addicted to drugs but remarkably, at the end of the day, he managed to kick the habit. My drinking stopped before I got hooked.

And then came the day when he appeared in my room, waving a newspaper at me. A conventional paper, not a scientific journal, or something of a more serious kind.

He pointed with his long bony fingers, which reflected his thin, upright body, rising to a height of 1.88 metres.

I read, and I was stunned.

The paper quoted from research conducted in Canada by some expert in D.N.A., who had succeeded in proving that Jews have a special, and unmistakable, form of D.N.A. This scientist had travelled to India and to Africa and on the basis of reliable tests had proved that among both Indians and Africans there are large numbers of Jews who have no inkling of their Jewish identity.

"Yes," I said, "I know Hitler used to claim that Jews have the blood of Negroes."

"Then I expect you know there was Jewish blood flowing in Hitler's veins too," Amin commented with undisguised pleasure.

"I've heard that one as well," I declared, hinting that I had neither the interest nor inclination to go wallowing in the putrid mire of a conversation on this subject or anything like it.

Amin took the hint, but he didn't change the subject and didn't leave my room.

"There's something else here," he added emphatically, as if to inform me that the "something else" was of the greatest importance, and he had not the shadow of a doubt that it would arouse my interest. Perhaps he was right. I listened to his theory.

"If Jews have different D.N.A., it should be possible to cultivate a micro-organism that will adapt and become dependent on the D.N.A. of Jews only. And if this micro-organism is malignant, it will attack and kill Jews. Only Jews. If the Germans had been a bit smarter, they wouldn't have needed all those cumbersome camps of theirs…"

"That really is a diabolical idea!" I couldn't resist responding.

He was silent.

"And you're going to try this?"

"Perhaps this is my mission on the earth!" he declared.

"A diabolical mission!" I exclaimed.

"That's a kind of mission too," he replied, sticking to his guns and making no attempt at compromise. And without hesitation he began setting out his plan before me.

It was based on the adaptation of *Rickettsia rickettsii*, the micro-organism that causes Rocky Mountain spotted fever, which has the same rate of lethality, i.e. 90%, as P. Pestis itself, the bacterium which apparently caused serious plagues in the Middle Ages and succeeding years and exterminated a third of the world's population at that time, except that the micro-organism in those days did not adapt and did not acquire a dependence on particular D.N.A.

"This time it will be different," Amin assured me as if donning the cloak of a comforter.

"It's going to cost you a fortune, doing that."

"My benefactors are prepared to invest however much is needed."

"Some benefactors!" I tried to inject a note of sarcasm into my reply, but I doubt I even managed mild scorn.

It occurred to me that if I were to go into the kitchen, choose a sharp and long-bladed knife and plunge it into Amin's heart, I might perhaps prevent disaster befalling the people among whom, by the will of fate, I was numbered. A patriot? I didn't see myself as a patriot. And however strange it may sound – I felt concerned for this idiot, Amin Abu Halil, who would be remembered as an eternal disgrace both among his own people and his "benefactors".

"You're taking on yourself something that will bring grief to you, to the whole of humanity and most important of all, bring grief to your own people, that you're so proud of," I said everything that was in my heart and felt relief as the idea of the long and sharp-bladed knife from the kitchen passed out of my consciousness.

And perhaps, I'm not flesh and blood and spirit and heart, animated by honour and a sense of responsibility, but just a little coward.

Amin Abu Halil rose from his seat, held out his bony hand to me, something he didn't do often, if at all. I shook the outstretched hand and he surprised me yet again, saying in pure Hebrew: "Shalom!"

I echoed him: "Shalom!"

He added in English: "I'm leaving now. It's been nice knowing you."

"For me too," I answered him.

And that was how we parted.

The report in the paper was as follows:

The new, integrated village of Hasda caused a worldwide sensation in its time, and perhaps also encouraged dreams of peace and an end to violence and hatred between Jews and Arabs. It was established, unlike anything that had gone before, on an Arab initiative, with Saudi support, both overt and covert, as an experiment in shared living between Jews and Arabs. Ten young families, most of them offspring of the Peace Now movement, on the extreme Left of Israeli politics, came to live there. Each family was given a house and a large patch of land, which they were obliged to cultivate and cherish, among the similar houses and gardens of the Arabs. At first nothing special was heard about the practical development of the place, and there was a general feeling that "no news is good news".

A few years before the foundation of the village of Hasda, a settlement known as Neve Shalom or "Groves of Peace" had been set up by Father Bruno, a Catholic monk, with financial support from American and other Jews, on land owned by the Trappist monastery of Latrun. The monk wanted to unite the three monotheistic religions. He worked day and night, travelled to countries all over the world, preached sermons, delivered impassioned speeches, clarified specific points, showed maps and plans for the construction of a multi-faith university, which would unite once and for all, from a religious and spiritual perspective, believers in the three monotheistic religions.

On a bare hillside buildings were erected and allocated to Jews, Arabs and Maronite Christians. The whole enterprise soon collapsed, and services in the mosque, the synagogue and the church no longer took place, and were not attended by visitors from all over the world, as Father Bruno had hoped and believed.

"Groves of Peace" died the kiss of death. No one mourned it. The zealous Father Bruno, a convert from Judaism of French origin, died along with the great project to which he had dedicated the rest of his life. If I'm not mistaken, he is buried on the crest of the hill. His rotting bones are all that remain of the brave dream.

CHAPTER FOUR

At eight in the morning, Swiss time, there was a call from reception. My wife took the call, heard whatever she heard, turned to me and announced: "Someone called Shmulik Landau from Israel wants to talk to you. The subject, he says, is urgent and pressing, from any angle."

I picked up the receiver.

"Who is this?"

"Shmulik. Shmulik Landau. The sergeant-major on the manoeuvres in Ze'elim, about ten years ago. You still don't remember?"

"I remember!" I answered him.

"We need you, urgently. I'm sure you've read the paper."

"I've read it," I confirmed.

"When are we going to see you here?"

"In about a month. To be more precise, twenty-eight days."

"I don't think you've understood what I'm saying," he responded, adding, "We need you urgently!"

"Who's this 'we'?"

"Your homeland... Incidentally, that song you composed, *King's Bride*, is something unique, it isn't so much a song as a hymn."

"A hymn to the brotherhood of the new Israel!" I filled it in for him.

"As for the singer, your wife has excelled herself with the new song: she's proved that it's still possible to reach astonishing heights. If you're sincere in your creations and steadfast in what you're conveying to your readers and listeners, you must leave Switzerland at once and stand alongside us..."

"Who exactly is this 'us'?" I pressed him further.

"Don't play the innocent," he replied, "you know what I'm involved with."

"I know," I answered him. I sensed my voice dropping, and he noticed this. I had no desire to make him plead.

"So what's stopping you coming and playing your part, however modest it may be, in solving the big problem that has been created... I'm sure you remember what you told us back then... during the manoeuvres..."

I remembered, but I saw no reason to bring up the subject again and think it through...

"I have obligations," I retorted.

"To whom?" my interlocutor wasn't giving up that easily. A metallic voice, of someone used to giving commands and not getting evasive answers.

"My wife," I replied, firmly.

"Your wife will be left by herself for just two days. You'll come here and go back. At the expense of the homeland and for its sake. Explain it to her. I haven't a shadow of a doubt she'll understand, and realise straightaway that you're trying to evade your responsibilities and in fact you're turning into a defeatist, a typical Diaspora Jew..." He tried insults as a way of undermining my stance but it wasn't working. I was too experienced to fall for that.

"It's out of the question," I declared, knowing how much this would annoy him.

"Is that your last word?" In the question there was a warning, a threat, pressure, and a demonstration of total lack of consideration, which was perfectly understandable and, no more and no less – justified. This made me angry.

"That is my last word."

"If that's the case," Shmulik declared, "I'll be seeing you tomorrow."

"You don't know where I am."

"Tell me."

"I'm not revealing my whereabouts, on principle," I replied.

"A fine principle," he told me approvingly. "You stick to it. But I'll find you. Don't be ridiculous. How do you think I got to you, and

I'm speaking to you now? Sleep well tonight and I'll be seeing you." End of conversation.

My wife was burning with a curiosity that was not to be doused until she heard all she wanted to hear, demanded to hear in fact, a silent, stern demand that could not be resisted, willingly or unwillingly, consciously or otherwise.

About ten years ago, I began telling the story, I took part in manoeuvres, as director of a laboratory in a field hospital. We set up the hospital in the desert of Ze'elim. And when I say 'we set it up' you have to understand it literally. The whole team was involved, everyone from the hospital director, a world-famous expert in brain surgery, through all the medical staff, doctors, nurses, orderlies, the duty chemist and your husband too, down to the last of the stretcher carriers. We erected huge tents, crammed in beds, which were nothing more than stretchers on trestles. I had to set up the laboratory tent myself, with minimal assistance. I took delivery of a heavy chest, made of wood and containing all the equipment and materials needed for the lab. Then we were told that the sergeant-major in charge of the hospital was intent on doing everything to ensure the success of the exercise, meaning, he would allow no officer, medical or otherwise, to sleep on the stretchers; they were expected to sleep on the solid ground of the desert, with no mattresses or anything resembling mattresses. It was clearly explained that the hospital sergeant-major was a young man, of very rigid personality and with experience of imposing order and discipline, who had proved himself in difficult situations, baulked at nothing and without a shadow of doubt, was liable to pounce on the most minor of infractions. Rumour had it, it wasn't worth tangling with this sergeant-major from any point of view.

This was not to my liking at all. Night came down. The signal was given. And all the personnel of the field hospital were required to bed down on the rocky ground of the Ze'elim desert. I sat in the lab tent, for which I was responsible. I lay down on the box of equipment and materials, and waited for the sergeant-major to arrive. Time crawled at the speed of a snail crossing dry ground. I stood up and went wandering around among the other tents, peered into the biggest tent where the doctors, in spite of the stern warnings, were lying down in the places reserved for theoretical patients. And then I saw a tall, erect young man, with an athletic build and an air of unassailable self-confidence, coming in by the other entrance to the tent. He approached the doctor closest to that entrance, leaned over him, asked his name and with the utmost civility, commanded him to get down immediately and lie on the ground... The doctor tried to say something, the charismatic young man simply repeated the word "immediately!" with dryness sharp as a scalpel and the doctor obeyed. So he went from doctor to doctor and soon had them all down on the ground.

I left the tent and the degrading treatment of those officer-doctors, humiliated before my eyes by that impertinent, ignorant young man, who had no sense of decorum whatsoever.

He came to the lab tent and found the acting director lying prone on the box of equipment and materials, which was locked and bolted.

"Get down from that box at once!" – his metallic voice cut through the stuffy air in that small tent.

"Who are you, Sir?" I asked him innocently.

"Sergeant-Major Shmuel Landau."

"Pleased to meet you!" I responded, told him my name and added, "Director of the laboratory."

"Please doctor," the energetic young man promoted me in the interests of achieving his objective, "tomorrow you can hand over the equipment, and the day after you can go home," – encouraging, logical statements, saying clearly, don't start getting awkward with me in the last few days of your reserve service, you're a sensible man! Please be so kind as to get down off the box and lie on the ground like all your colleagues!

"With pleasure, esteemed Sergeant-Major,

Shmuel Landau, on one explicit condition – you sign the transfer chit for me here and now, and take full responsibility for the contents of this box, which include precious and delicate items such as microscopes, as well as substances which junkies would be only too glad to get their hands on and consume. I'm sure you're aware that among the stretcher bearers there are at least five known drug addicts, currently in rehab. Are you prepared to sign for all this?"

A broad, bright, surprising smile spread over the intense, intelligent face and loosened the habitually tight lips, and Sergeant-Major Shmuel left the lab tent. So I slept on the box that night and the nights that followed. My back was not scratched by the sharp stones of the desert. In the morning, Shmuel visited me again, and went on visiting. From the 96% proof alcohol that was freely available, and fresh lemon juice, I mixed a superior cocktail; the hospital personnel, especially the doctors and some of the admin officers, used to come and plead for a glass. So we began gathering, without any prior intention, in the tent assigned to me. And everyone would talk of his experiences to those seated around, while sipping the potent, natural liquor, which guaranteed, after the third glass, the absolute separation from his surroundings that everyone longed for. On one such occasion I mentioned my friendship with Amin Abu Halil and his ingenious idea, a way of putting an end to the Jewish race by means of pure microbiology, an elegant and economical process. The listeners, Shmulik among them, were stunned, and two litres of booze disappeared among them without anyone noticing. It seemed Sergeant-Major Shmulik remembered that strange story he heard from me some years before, when he read, as I did, the newspaper story, and tied up the loose ends.

Incidentally, a persistent rumour held that Shmulik had been transferred to counter-intelligence services, and everyone who heard this and knew anything of him, had not the slightest doubt that in view of his determination, acute intellect and other similar qualities – this was the right place for him.

The next day, early in the morning, there was a call from hotel reception: a man called Shmulik Landau was demanding to see me urgently, and I knew how justified this demand was. He was waiting for me in the hotel lobby and wasn't going to budge from there until I had been kind enough to go down and see him.

My reply was positive. I dressed, washed my face and hurried down to reception, where a surprise awaited me. In one of the armchairs, with its friendly beige upholstery, sat a man who could definitely be described as handsome, in a grey tailored suit. He rose to meet me, looking every inch the English gentleman.

"Your weekend leave has been cancelled!" he declared in his limpid, typically sharp voice, and saw fit to explain: "You haven't shaved!"

"Sergeant-Major Landau!" I responded in the same tone. "You said you wanted to see me urgently."

"There's always time to shave. Consider yourself confined to barracks, as of this moment."

I invited him into the hotel restaurant. He asked for coffee. I ordered decaffeinated for myself.

"High blood pressure?" asked Shmulik.

"Just the way I prefer it," I answered him.

"You've read the papers?"

I nodded.

"I'm sure you can shed some light on the case. And you can tell us about the guy who came up with the idea, Amin Abu Halil – your friend from way back."

I nodded again.

"First things first, and last things last," I began and detected a hint of tension in the muscles of the long face, a face radiating knowledge and confidence and so it seemed, under strict control, and this reassured me. "As for the disease itself, I can tell you exactly what's involved."

From some hidden pocket he drew out a thick notebook with a tiny ballpoint pen attached to the side. He opened the notebook, and sat pen in hand, ready to record: "It's a disease popularly known in English as Rocky Mountain spotted fever." He made a careful note of this and I added frankly: "I'm sorry to say, there is no cure for it. The mortality rate is very high – 90%," I told him, and he wrote this down too. "It's important to keep up the strength of patients affected by it – vitamins, fluids, strict personal hygiene. The cause: *Rickettsia rickettsii*, a bacterium transmitted by the ticks that infest animals. Doctors will no doubt be rushing to consult their textbooks, and with a bit of luck, it may be some antidote has been developed, since the time when the disease was revealed and correctly diagnosed."

He wrote it all down.

"As for Amin Abu Halil, we were friends, close friends, you could say. He has an obsessive idea, he wants to finish off the job that Hitler started and if he's been successful – as the reports in the media suggest – there's hardly anything that can be done to stop him."

"We want you to talk to him, probe, find out how far things have gone. We've tracked him down, and he's living in Berlin, Humboldt Strasse, number 19. He's married to a German woman, Hilda, granddaughter of a Nazi general, who committed suicide along with Hitler when the Reich collapsed. We're sending you there at our expense, flying business class, five star hotel..."

"I'll do it with pleasure," I answered him, "as soon as my holiday is over, in about three weeks from now... as I told you. I shall shoulder my responsibilities."

"Is your wife upstairs?" – he arched a thick eyebrow towards the ceiling.

I nodded.

"Let me talk to her for a quarter of an hour."

"I'd rather you didn't."

"Why?"

"She'll feel pressurised. Three weeks from now – I'll be all yours."

He sipped his coffee and I sipped mine, which had gone cold.

"I've been in Bulgaria."

"What took you to Bulgaria?" I asked, my curiosity aroused.

"I was dredging up information about you. I found the man you call 'Vladimir' in *Erral* – that autobiographical book of yours. His real name is Ermencho. I introduced myself and I have to say, the Bulgarians have a lot of respect for Israel's intelligence services."

"They're not the only ones," I commented.

He acknowledged this with a nod of the head, and went on to say:

"I got an authentic profile from him. He said, it was nice working with you, you have a 'lively mind' as he put it, a talent for improvisation, and he also described you in a way you won't like: a Jewish intellect, as opposed to a Bulgarian intellect, which he calls 'square', doing everything possible to imitate the German intellect and, regrettably, to resemble it. He asked me most earnestly to pass on his apologies, about the way you parted company in Prague, and the offence that he caused you on your most sensitive point – Judaism. He called this your strong and your weak point. You became a communist to fight the 'enemy' of the Jews and not for reasons of pure ideology, as they would have liked. It's very easy to get you riled, with the lightest of touches on the Jewish button. He asked if it's our intention to recruit you for some specific mission in the highly respected Israeli intelligence service, which he meant as a compliment. My honest answer was yes."

"Is this an offer?" I asked him.

"You could see it that way," he declared.

"You know I've retired."

"Oh, of course," Shmulik confirmed and added as if trying to offer a bribe: "A man like you shouldn't be just sitting there, flicking channels between TV, video and DVD screens, your place is to cause the events that will happen and direct them, not look on from the sidelines."

"You don't know me," I protested.

"That's where you're mistaken. We got to know each other inside and out in those manoeuvres," and he added, moving on to specifics: "You are the only one, since that time to this day, out of all my subordinates, including men of remarkable guile, wit and wisdom, not to mention avowed delinquents – who has failed to obey my orders and not been punished for it. The one and only."

"That isn't enough!" I exclaimed.

"Let me be the judge of that!" he insisted firmly, emphatically.

"Do you want an immediate answer?" I asked, and succeeded in changing the subject, which seemed sterile to me.

"One of these days I'll demand that."

"And in the meantime?"

"Let's be content with what you can do now. For your country. This isn't a theatrical rendition" – he saw fit to stress:

"A new light gleams in the azure sky/ A breeze from the sea speeds over the plain/ Homeland of ours we love you / In peace, and in trouble and at war..." Shmulik recited the first verse of *King's Bride*, and added: "It's a long time since a song like that has been written. And I'm absolutely sure you have no intention of repudiating it."

"That isn't in my nature," I replied.

"I know!" He sank into a meaningful silence and then spoke again: "We'll let you finish your holiday." He rose to his feet. Tall, athletic, well-mannered and utterly fearless, a people with sons like this will not easily be defeated. He held out to me a visiting-card, with his name in blue letters in a blue surround and telephone numbers in black. "When you're ready, call me!" he said, "And don't forget to pass on my sincere admiration to your wife." He stretched out an elegant hand; his handshake was frank, warm and wise. We parted. I had taken a few steps when suddenly an idea flashed into my mind, and I turned and ran after him. Shmulik heard me running, stopped, turned and waited.

"Something occurred to you?" he asked, saving me my opening words.

"Yes," I replied. "To make this despicable project work, the micro-organism known as *Rickettsia*, or more precisely *Rickettsia rickettsii*" – he repeated the terms after me, trying to imprint these weird names in his memory – "has to be fed with the blood of Jews. Is that clear so far?"

"Clear!" he confirmed in a manner leaving no room for doubt.

"That means," I went on to say, "the theft of large quantities of blood. Something you could try, is persuading the managers of blood-banks in hospitals, especially in the North, to check their stocks. I wouldn't be at all surprised if they were surprised by the results. Careful investigation will reveal who stole the blood – and the thread will lead to something deeper and infinitely more surprising."

"I've taken all that in, boss," Shmulik confirmed.

I returned to the hotel. My wife was waiting for me, tensed up to the very limit – and beyond. I changed my clothes and decided on pre-emptive action: "Right, I'll tell you what's going on."

The tension eased, as I told her. It seemed the story appealed to her. She had always been a fan of detective novels and suspense films.

"Now I believe the stories you told me about the 'combat squads' and your activities as a member of them."

"Don't you think that's a rather insulting remark?" I asked.

"No," she protested. "It isn't easy to believe all the stories you tell me."

"That's been my mistake."

"What has?"

"Telling you."

"Doesn't every male try to impress his woman? Your behaviour is normal. And I don't mean to offend you, and you haven't taken offence, have you?" she asked with disarming, irresistible innocence.

"Absolutely not!" – a heartfelt, two-word closing statement, clarifying everything.

"And do you think you'll take up the offer?" she asked.

"No," was my candid reply.

"Perhaps all the same you could make some

contribution," she suggested.

"I can do that without being drafted. The nice thing about retirement is that they stop pestering you with instructions and demands. If they want the benefit of my accumulated experience, they're welcome to it. And that's the best for both parties."

"But you won't be paid for it."

"With the pension, and the extra income from writing and recording royalties – in particular what you bring in – we have enough and to spare!" I declared in a tone to brook no contradiction.

My wife considered this and agreed: "You're absolutely right!"

Two weeks later, there were reports in the papers, on radio and the visual media too, of a perplexing incident which had occurred in a hospital in Nahariyya; a twelve year old Arab boy, seriously injured in a road accident, had been admitted and he needed an emergency blood transfusion. His blood type, AB, Rh(-) was a rare one, but according to the list of types available in the hospital, there was supposed to be a supply of it in the blood-bank. To the surprise of the doctors, it turned out there was none there, and the child died in their hands. An enquiry revealed that a quantity of AB, Rh(-) was kept for urgent cases and so it was listed, but it was not to be found in the special refrigeration unit where it was stored. A police investigation concluded that the blood had been stolen. Rumour had it that Arabs from Upper Galilee had started stealing blood, for no discernible purpose. It turned out that stocks of other types of blood were missing too, despite the meticulous lists that were kept, and these were not necessarily the rare types. The grandfather of the boy who had died, Muhammad Nabulsi, a cleaner at the hospital for many years, went to the police and confessed that fanatical underground types had demanded that he hand over to them stocks of blood from the hospital, which they needed, and if not, they threatened to kill him and his family. To the question, did they demand supplies of blood of rare types, Mr Nabulsi admitted that this was not the case, but in his foolish way of thinking, as he put it himself, he decided that the rare types, kept in a separate fridge, would be of more interest to the blackmailers, and so this was what he did and Allah had punished him and his beloved grandson had paid with his life for his conduct, which ill befitted a Muslim. When asked if he was afraid that those fanatics would carry out their threat and kill him, the man replied that this no longer mattered to him, and he was praying that God would forgive the evil he had done and his life was worthless to him now; he would try to mend his ways and beg to be forgiven, since he did what he did in innocence of heart, and God sees, as no other can, the inner thoughts of the human heart, and He is compassionate and merciful.

The police investigation continued, and it was discovered that stocks of blood had been stolen from the hospital in Haifa too, but of common types. An Arab cleaning lady and her two assistants had been arrested. The motive behind the thefts remained obscure.

CHAPTER FIVE

As is the natural way, things began to calm down. We went out every day to stroll around Zurich, which we had come to know well. We didn't often find a restaurant that suited us. Japanese, Chinese, Thai, Greek, Turkish, Arab restaurants – all had long ago lost their exotic charm. It seemed they only kept going on the basis of European boredom and the restlessness of people who go away on expensive holidays, and pensioners whose pensions, in thrifty hands, enable them to wander the world far and wide and experience all its wonders, before the fleshly eyes that are always yearning and never satisfied are closed, the questing heart is stilled, and the tongue and the palate are no longer serviceable for experiencing, seeing, expounding, hearing, probing and tasting, however much is possible.

We tried out quite a few specifically non-exotic restaurants, including large self-service establishments.

On the Bahnhoff Strasse, the central thoroughfare of Zurich, stand three gigantic department stores, each comprising grocery shops on the lower ground floor, on the level above it sales of household and kitchen supplies, in all their varieties and eccentricities; on the upper floor – clothing, and on the roof – a huge self-service restaurant. "Manor" for the paupers, "Co-op" for the petty bourgeois, "Jelmoli" for the snobs. And finally, "Migros", a popular establishment combining Italian speakers, Italian style, Italian food and Italian prices.

It is only right to stress the high standard of the emphatically Swiss and well maintained toilets operating in each of the above-mentioned establishments, located, for public convenience, on the upper floor, and constituting a part of the restaurant. Sometimes, those requiring toilets come up without needing anything else, not even a glass of water, and this in all weathers, and they praise the consummate, socio-humane concept. As a whole, at regular times, regular people arrive at regular places. Once it happened that my wife needed to do some repairs to her clothing, on a cold and wet day, but had no means of doing this. Naturally, all the regular visitors to the café-restaurant were witnesses to her futile attempts to do what she wanted to do but was incapable of doing. And then, a middle-aged woman rose from her regular seat, approached us and proffered a pair of folding scissors, which as it turned out, she always carried around with her in her handbag specifically for cases such as these, and the business was settled in the most heart-warming way.

It was not by mere coincidence that Peter Kropotkin, the eminent anarchist, gained the initial impression that "people are good" by their very nature and tend to help one another – in Switzerland certainly, it is down to the behaviour of the Swiss.

CHAPTER SIX

According to a principle, which we adhere to, we don't watch television and we don't even have a set at home. In our hotel room, the TV is tempting, with all its dumb innocence and unhypocritical humility. And it turns out that every year programmes about sport are aired, and those who understand sport or enjoy watching it need have no fear of being bored. I never liked sport of any kind; the principles behind it and the objectives mean nothing to me. But here I was in for a surprise. My wife proved to be an avid fan of sports programmes, identifying with the competitors, and sometimes breaking into spontaneous applause in front of the screen. She claimed that by observing the facial expression of each competitor, and in particular his level of determination, she could predict who was going to win the contest and indeed, it was just as she said. I commented that if it were possible to bet on these contests in the same way as on horse races, we could recoup the full cost of our holiday.

In high school I was renowned for my avoidance of physical education classes, to the point where the tolerant and genial P.E. teacher was driven to distraction, threatening to ruin my "average" by marking me down in his subject. His wrath, utterly at odds with his pleasant personality and mild manner, blazed so fiercely that he took the trouble to invent a new rating, hitherto unknown in any school in Bulgaria, or elsewhere. My mark in the subject of physical education was a big round "0" – zero. And because this original and creative mark had no verbal definition, it stayed on my record in its primal form, from the ninth to the twelfth grade.

And here I had to suffer, and it was real physical suffering – on account of this particular penchant of my wife, not quite feminine in my humble opinion. (I told her this repeatedly and with excessive emphasis, but to no avail.) My wife would run to the set, switch it on and sit down facing the screen as if hypnotised, at all hours of the day. And just as passive smoking can lead to passive nicotine poisoning, so there are lethal passive toxins in television-watching, especially if two people are together in the confined space of a hotel room, for hour after hour, as the set exudes its poison. To me, the whole business looks primitive, at best infantile.

Running long distances, winning medals, and indulging in perverted national pride. And what about all those who haven't won medals? And the most important accolade is providing the excuse for the playing of the national anthem of the state that you represent. As the anthem is being played, a carefully regulated scenario is taking place. Facing the medal-winner, on a tall mast, his country's flag is hoisted. He fixes his gaze on it, in serious and well rehearsed style, as if seeing it for the first time in his life, and as the first note of the anthem rings out, both his eyes, simultaneously fill with clearly visible moisture. Only Russian women have invented an alternative scenario for themselves, more convenient and more appropriate to their semi-Asiatic temperament. One of them, from Belarus, started weeping while the flag was still being hoisted, and when the piece of coloured cloth reached the top of the mast, the lady broke into such a paroxysm of sobs that her neighbours on the podium had to support her, lest she collapse under the weight of her emotion. Truly, an infantile display of an infantile phenomenon. I almost learned the American anthem by heart, as it was played with such frequency, dutifully serenading the American athletes, waving their medals for the cameras. I learnt it in a dispassionate way, not at all willingly. Passive viewing.

I also filled some gaps in my knowledge,

since were it not for sport, of which my wife turned out to be an enthusiastic devotee, I would not have known that the Bahamas have a national anthem. Admittedly, the Bahamian anthem was played only once, as were, at best, the original anthems of other countries similar to it. Not one of them has stuck in my memory.

Female tennis players, despite all the hard work, vision and artistry invested in their tough and exhausting game, cherish a reservoir of blind hatred for one another, and if it were possible to attack one another, there is not a shadow of doubt that without the slightest twinge of conscience, they would rip out their rivals' eyes with their fingernails.

And something else: in sport there are competitors and rivals, but no "partners" or "colleagues". From an educational point of view, it would be very desirable to ban certain games, which are not games but a distant relic of gladiatorial combat and the kind of effervescent venomous hatred, primitive and lethal, that people try in vain to cope with. And here is sport, nourishing it as a poisonous snake nourishes her offspring.

My wife showed a lively and inexorable interest in a tennis player of Swiss origin, Roger Federer. I felt obliged to take an interest in him too, and once again I was made aware of my wife's superior tastes, and this is not just self-congratulation.

This young man is remarkable for some rare traits of personality, including an impressive degree of humility, alongside generosity and commitment to the objective, namely victory achieved not for the sake of self-aggrandisement. He plays the creative game of a white prince of sport. And he always wins. And it seems to me, that his competitors feel respect for him if in spite of themselves, and in some sense are proud of the privilege of playing against him. And if I'm wrong about this, I would advise them to take it up. Naturally, not all of them. The negative version of Federer are two players who for some reason appear in white gear, without inspiration or the slightest hint of taste or an aesthetic approach. The older, Mr Agassi, stands out for his obsequious and theatrical playing to the crowd: bowing, blowing kisses and on the other hand spitting out snot with a finger over one nostril, like a janitor in an abattoir. The other, of inflated ego, is Kiffer. Both of them have won a number of games, displaying all the petty-mindedness of traders in haberdashery and second-hand clothing – a profession infinitely more appropriate for them than the game of tennis, in which Roger Federer holds sway. Thanks to my wife I took an interest in him, an interest which began in those days and is finishing today, at this hour, with this sentence, with this full-stop.

CHAPTER SEVEN

And then came another blow, which could not in any way have been envisaged, one of those things which happen when people go away on holiday.

One day my wife got up and announced, with all the seriousness and maturity which distinguish her, that she could not see. Incapable of reading a newspaper or watching television. We made an appointment with an optometrist and paid him eight hundred Swiss francs, ready cash. There are 3.6 shekels to a franc. My wife was treated to a lengthy explanation of the defect that had shown up in her eyesight, and as always happens with medical consultations in the private sector, she was told she had arrived at the very last moment – any more delay and her eyesight would have been severely endangered and the rest of her life turned to tragedy. On our return from the optometrist, my wife asked, did the professional expert mean that she would need a white stick wherever she went in the world.

I tried to reassure her.

"I'm right beside you!" I declared with excessive confidence. She clutched my arm and almost wept with emotion.

Sure enough, the next day we went and received two pairs of gleaming spectacles. My wife was euphoric.

After a few hours of gazing at the splendid world of the Holy One blessed be He, through one of those pairs and a hasty attempt to read a newspaper standing up, my wife again declared she could see nothing, could not pick out objects or letters.

We returned to the optometrist. He repeated the process and checked everything with commendable thoroughness, and found that in the laboratory his instructions had not been properly followed and there had been confusion. He promised that the issue would be rectified fully and expeditiously, and we were asked to come back the next day. Early in the morning we presented ourselves, and were given repaired spectacles. My wife's mouth was filled with all the praises in the world. We reached the hotel, and the phenomenon repeated itself – no distant sight, letters at close range illegible. As I write these lines, we are planning yet another visit to the professional and may God be with us.

CHAPTER EIGHT

We went down to Lake Zurich. The temperature was cool, without being threatening, the climate for which we flew to Switzerland in the first place and which we didn't always get. We walked with the stream of pedestrians and bicycle riders on the broad promenade alongside the lake. People smiled at one another. If someone smiled broadly at someone smiling at him, this was interpreted as an invitation to conversation and so on. We didn't need this. We reached the end of the promenade and returned, slowing our steps, filling our lungs with invigorating, oxygenated air. We returned the way we had come, walked over the broad bridge crossing the garden where on Saturdays a flea-market was held. We made slow progress, finally arriving at "Sprüngli", a European café of petty bourgeois flavour, famous for its homemade cakes and chocolate, not only in Switzerland but outside it as well.

"Sprüngli" had tables on the pavement and also a large room on the upper floor. We decided to sit outside under the parasols, designed to provide shade from the sun and now affording some protection from the light rain. Before we sat down the rain started falling, adding to the ozone and to the pleasure of the excursion. A waitress in a classic, starched-white Viennese apron approached us, bowed lightly and stylishly and asked what we wanted. We ordered what we ordered and it was served within less than five minutes. We sipped "Sprüngli's" excellent cappuccino with deep enjoyment, that concoction which my wife, in her exalted mood, described as a "masterpiece". The rain was merciful to us and didn't strengthen, while the pink parasol protected us and contributed to the boosting of our spirits. And then we both noticed, with our peripheral vision, and from our separate places, two guys standing by the open-air counter and staring at us. Young men, in Swiss suits like those worn by bank-clerks and schoolteachers. After about two minutes the shorter of the two approached us and asked if the two chairs next to us were free. We couldn't say "No", though we would have liked to. It isn't the Swiss way to refuse to accommodate people who want to share a table, rather the opposite. I hurriedly nodded my head, not wanting to give the impression that the dwarfish young man had broken my wife's heart. The one who approached us thanked us in clear German, signalled to his friend to come over and the two of them sat down facing us. The waitress arrived, took their order, brought two cups of steaming coffee. I began chatting with my wife in as animated a style as possible, hoping to convey the message that we weren't looking for new interlocutors. We spoke English. This surprised the two men, and the dwarf addressed me again, asking in English as deformed as himself, the most hackneyed question of all: where were we from.

The atmosphere was not pleasant, and the expressions on the faces of the two contributed to our unease. The dwarf could have been a sergeant in the Wermacht, with his ruddy face and big dark eyes in constant movement back and forth, like the eyes of an animal in a cartoon film. The tall, thin one was reminiscent of one of Hitler's more spectacularly stupid generals, only his childlike devotion to his Fuhrer rendering him photogenic to a certain extent. It seemed he knew about photography, as he said a few words about cameras, enlargements and lenses. At a certain moment, chosen by me, I lied to the dwarf about our origins:

"My wife is American," I said, "and I'm Bulgarian." It wasn't such a big lie: I was born in that country and its language was my mother-tongue, while my wife had spent a fair number of her years in the land of the buffalo and the

Red Indian and the Hollywood soap opera, and she spoke fluent American. She took the initiative, turned to me and said:

"Let's not forget, the Schwarzewald family are supposed to be visiting with us today."

I put on a serious face, agreed with her at once, signalled to the waitress who was exceptionally alert to hints such as these, and was standing beside me just a moment later, one hand in the leather money-belt at her waist, rummaging among the assorted notes and coins. We paid.

"Just a moment," the dwarf said as if suddenly waking up, "we know which way you're going, and we'd be happy to give you a lift to your hotel. We have a nice VW Beetle outside. You can see, the rain has no intention of stopping, on the contrary – it's getting stronger."

My wife turned to me, looking for a response. Her eyes said – find us a way out of this! I found one:

"We prefer to use the tram. Thanks all the same."

Here the thin one intervened, saying:

"Think about it for a moment! You can hear the rain and the wind. It's no trouble to us. We're going to the same destination."

"We appreciate your offer, Herr..."

"Obermann" – he filled it in for me, listening intently to every syllable I uttered, and forcing me to weigh every letter before articulating it.

"It's been a great pleasure meeting you, Herr Obermann!" I declared and almost clicked my heels, in the style of long-dead officers of the Reich.

We moved towards the street. At that moment, a Number 11 stopped. We both ran, the rain catching up with us every other step. We boarded the tram, found dry seats, and relaxed, taking deep gulps of invigorating, therapeutic air. Half an hour later, we were in our tidy, spotlessly clean hotel room. On the table, a couple of ripe apples and two small bars of chocolate. We attacked them without mercy, till nothing was left but the chocolate wrappers, discarded in the bin. My wife was agitated.

"You saw!" – she pronounced the exclamation mark.

"There's nothing to be done. That's what comes of going for a walk with a woman as attractive as you!"

"Leave out the Stone Age wise-cracks. They know where we're staying."

"That doesn't bother me."

"I don't know why you're being so casual about this."

"What is it about this whole episode that you find strange?"

She repeated emphatically, her voice quivering a little:

"They know where we're staying. They know us but we don't know them."

"I don't mind not knowing them," I replied in a melodious voice, like a bird set free from a cage. My wife went to the window, and suddenly let out a cry, something not characteristic of her.

"Look!" she said pointing. I rushed to her side, looked, and saw.

Someone was pointing a telescopic camera at me. I wasted no time, putting the thumb of one hand to the end of my nose, the other thumb on the little finger, and moved my hands this way and that in a gesture of contempt, intending to annoy and generally succeeding. Without expressing any opinion of me, my wife put on a raincoat and ran to the lift. I followed her example and caught up with her. We went down in the lift and to the edge of the field adjoining the hotel, and possibly belonging to it, where the pair of clowns we met at "Sprüngli" were standing, their faces expressing despair hard to gauge, like two buffoons who have blundered in a popular farce and are exposed to the scorn and derision of the audience.

"Get out of here!" my wife shouted, though she had no legal right to demand this. The tall one got into the Beetle, parked a few paces from us, put the telescopic camera away, picked up a conventional camera from the seat and without any shame, pointed it at me. My wife stooped and found something which I would never have imagined could be found in a Swiss field – certainly not a ploughed field, replete with germinating corn – a round stone, which was immediately flung at the tall man's face, to be more precise, at his camera, which a moment before had managed to click a few times, being held in the hands of an expert. The dwarf approached my wife, but I saw he had no fighting spirit in him, so I left him, for better or worse, to the tender mercies of her hands, which soon found, to the shame of the Swiss, two more round stones, hurled straight into the face of the dwarf. I ran towards the tall one, and did what they do in all the films – I tapped him lightly on the shoulder, and he obediently turned to me his Quixote-ish features. Two fleshless jaw-bones received one after the other four well-aimed punches, two apiece. He collapsed at my feet. I turned my attention to the dwarf, who in the meantime had managed to take refuge in the vehicle, and from there he waved an admonitory finger, sometimes in my wife's direction, sometimes in mine – the gesture of a prankster in a class of backward children. My wife approached Mr Obermann, still prostrate at my feet. From the inside pocket of his tailored jacket, peered the edge of a white piece of paper or card. She stooped and with a swift movement, pulled out something that looked like a visiting card. We read the content: written there in square Teutonic manuscript was the name of the hotel where we were staying, our room number, surname and first names. My wife exclaimed:

"That which I feared has come upon us!" – and put the card back in its place.

Without exchanging another word, we folded our tents and sounded the retreat. We ran up a hillock and soon we were back in our room. We took off our coats and flung them down on the upholstered chairs. My wife's face showed anxiety which could not be hidden or disregarded.

"What are you so worried about?" I asked her.

"They're looking for you," she replied.

"Why would they be looking for me?" I asked innocently.

"Stop playing games. Only you can foil their intentions."

"Who are *they*, and what intentions are you talking about?"

"Your Arab friend and his cronies!"

"Why should they do that?" I persisted.

"You're the only one who knows the material, the only one who can seriously jeopardise their nefarious schemes."

"They aren't that clever!" I declared, and hugged her shoulders.

"Your face is covered in mud!" my wife cried, with an expression of horror.

"So is yours!" I replied.

She smiled.
I ushered her into the bathroom.

CHAPTER NINE

In the media, especially in the papers and on television, worrying reports began to appear about natural disasters, and this time, unlike in previous times, Switzerland too was hit by severe floods. In the forests of Portugal giant fires raged, and there were victims. As happened every year, a hurricane threatened the coasts of America and China. The mood was gloomy, the air in the room was dense, and not easy to breathe.

After much hesitation and cogitation, my wife plucked up her courage and turned to me with a question:

"Why is this happening?"

We were sitting in the quiet room. Rain lashed the windows.

"There exists a divine justice," I began – "and it's a sure foundation for the balance of forces in nature. When this divine justice is impaired," I went on to explain, "the balance of natural forces is disrupted and the result: natural disasters, the source of which is – immoral behaviour. In the Bible it is written: For all flesh has corrupted his way (Genesis chapter six, verse twelve)."

"For example?"

"Incest. Not long ago we heard about a man who seduced a mother and her daughter, or the brother and sister, each of whom raised a family, and who then embarked on a sexual relationship with each other, and other cases that we haven't heard about, all of them constituting a serious offence against divine justice and a no less serious disruption of the balance of natural forces. The prophet Jonah, who refused to obey God and to fulfil his mission, offended against divine justice and disrupted the forces of nature. The ship on which Jonah meant to escape from his God, was on the point of breaking up and sinking along with all those on board. Jonah, whose faith was true, and whose trust in God was without flaw, called on those praying on the ship to throw him in the sea, as he was the reason for their disaster, he the one who offended against divine justice and disrupted the balance of natural forces, and they believed him and did as he asked, and the ship was saved with all hands. God rescued Jonah, his chosen and steadfast envoy."

"And what about the forest fires?" she

persisted.

"The same principle as for the floods."

"As far as I know," she continued, "the Jews have always been accused of offending against divine justice and disrupting the balance of natural forces, as you call them."

"The Jews are the only people in the world who are not content with not acknowledging Jesus Christ and not believing his message, but – unlike every other people, nation and race in the world – the Jewish race persecutes Jesus Christ, hates him and curses him, and this is a serious offence against divine justice and the balance of natural forces."

"And if the Jews stop persecuting, hating and cursing Jesus Christ, who incidentally was born and died a Jew – what will be the outcome?"

I replied with solid and unassailable confidence: "It will be the age of the salvation of the human race."

"Why do the Jews refuse to stop persecuting, hating and cursing Jesus Christ?"

"Why does the blind man not see the light, so that any small stone can trip him and bring him to the ground?"

"I don't think the Jews will ever abandon their blind behaviour."

"Then there will be no salvation for the human race, of which the Jews are a part."

"Why is a man born a Jew?"

"Why is an elephant born an elephant?"

"That isn't a fair analogy!" – a note of serious protest in her voice.

"One necessarily exists as does the other, so that divine justice will be revealed and the balance of natural forces maintained. Any thought, word or deed which offends, intentionally or otherwise, consciously or unconsciously, against divine justice and disrupts the balance of natural forces, resulting in natural disaster, is defined both in ancient and in modern Hebrew as a 'despicable act'."

"An apt definition!" – she expressed emphatic satisfaction. "And what your friend Amin is doing or planning to do, isn't that a 'despicable act'?"

"A despicable act in the first degree."

"But that hasn't caused any natural disasters."

"If that isn't stopped, it's going to bring about the murderous business called war."

CHAPTER TEN

I had a cousin, eight years older than me, articulate and well-mannered, shrewd although uneducated, not renowned for his diligence or for his conscientious approach to work. In the tradition of Jews of Spanish ancestry, he was named, as was I and a dozen other cousins on my father's side, Shlomo, after our grandfather.

In the place where I was born and grew up, sustaining a family was the mark of manhood, and more important still was the achievement of sustaining that family with integrity and honour. Also in the place where I was born, an acute economic crisis erupted, and thousands were thrown out into the street, without any source of income whatsoever. My cousin, may he rest in Paradise, was one of them. He had a family: a pleasant and sharp-witted wife, two wonderful children. Responsibility for the family was laid on him, and slowly but surely it became clear that he needed no help from relatives, and more than this, my cousin proved himself a man, in other words – he sustained his family with integrity and honour. Obviously not through his former profession, seriously damaged as a result of the economic crisis, or any other regular profession either. My shrewd cousin, with a total of four years of primary education behind him, sustained his family with integrity and honour, incredible as it may sound – by playing poker. We were good friends and enjoyed each other's company and conversation, so I suggested a meeting and asked him directly, as was customary between us: "Tell me, Cousin, do you really earn all your income in these turbulent times – from poker? And the big head with the tousled, dense and curly black hair, went down and up again, twice, in an abrupt movement. His vocal version of the answer was a resolute: "Yes!"

"But how can it be so?" I wondered. "I know you're a member of a poker club for factory managers, which was disbanded although it continues to meet secretly, and there, to the best of my knowledge, anyone caught cheating is thrown out. Final and irrevocable expulsion."

"They've never caught me cheating and they never will."

"So how is it that you always win?" I pressed him: "Can you explain?"

"Willingly!" he declared. "You're familiar with all the thirty-two cards. You see the cards dealt to you, remember the cards you've discarded and what replaced them. With a sidelong glance, often enough – you catch the edge of a card that's been discarded or has fallen, and you make your calculations, which aren't particularly complicated. You have a rough idea of who's holding what. You also know the personalities of the other players. There are the frivolous ones and the sensible ones, the pedantic and the broad-minded. All of this guarantees you an adequate return at the end of the working day, and we're talking one day a week."

"One day a week, i.e. four days a month, earns you enough to support a family of four, with honour and integrity?" I expressed my astonishment.

"Exactly so!" my cousin retorted, still miffed by the suspicions I had raised over cheating.

"But my dear Cousin," I persisted. "it still depends on the luck of the cards."

"You intellectuals call it the luck of the cards."

"And what do you call it?"

"By the right word and the true name."

"Which is?" – I wasn't letting up.

"God."

This was not a comfortable situation, since in that country there was a communist regime, and anyone mentioning the name of God aroused immediate suspicion and could expect his situation to become immeasurably more serious.

"Can you elucidate?" I asked.

"Gladly," my cousin replied and for the first time I felt he had got over the offence I had caused him with my suspicions. "You have to be worthy of God's attention."

"And that means?" I pressed him, conceding nothing but full of curiosity.

"Behaving as God wants you to behave."

"How?"

"Not lying, not deceiving, not cheating and most of all, being charitable."

"That's all there is to it then, being charitable?"

"Hardly a case of 'that's all there is to it'. You have to give with all your heart."

"For example?" I demanded an illustration and it was supplied at once.

"For example, you see one of the players in the game, in desperation, making a fatal mistake, and you can tell, just by looking at his face, that he's in a desperate financial plight and his family is destitute. There's a thousand dollars in the pot. You make an educated guess at which cards he's holding. You know for sure that with the cards you have, the pot is yours, but you fold all the same. You let him win and he takes the thousand dollars with a warm sense of achievement. You don't see yourself as a sucker, but on the contrary, you know for certain that your conduct is compatible with the will of God and you feel greatly relieved at heart. You even breathe more easily. You haven't strayed onto the slippery slope of chasing petty profit.

"God will refund you double, fourfold or more, whatever sum you donated to that poor sod, thereby giving him a few moments of happiness and satisfaction."

"And that's all?" I concluded, disappointed.

"That's all," he confirmed in his deep, throaty, manly voice.

"And what about all those duplicate packs and switching cards?" I knew I was offending him again.

"That's all!" he repeated emphatically in that throaty, deep voice, tempered by years of chain-smoking.

"May God be with you!" I blessed him, a strange thing for me to say in those days, and quite dangerous.

"And with you too," he replied and added: "Don't worry, you haven't got a dishonest cousin. Even in these hectic times, he's supporting his family with integrity and honour. And if you ever need a loan, don't be shy about approaching your cousin."

He arrived in Israel with his family, didn't find work, but did find poker enthusiasts like himself, and continued to practise his bizarre profession. Sometimes he was invited to the homes of poker fanatics, and usually went away satisfied, with a clear profit, leaving behind him among his fellow players not the slightest trace of a suspicion that they had been duped.

One Sabbath, leaving a house in which a game had taken place, with twelve thousand dollars in his pocket, he was knocked down by a drunk driver and killed instantly. His body was taken to the pathology lab, and was returned the following day to his wife and two children. Everything was intact – identity papers, small change. Of the money that he won, those twelve thousand dollars in hard cash, not a cent was found on his body.

His family and fellow players saw no point in claims and investigations; it was agreed that these "would not bring the dead back to life".

May he rest in Paradise! This chapter is a modest memorial to him.

CHAPTER ELEVEN

We strolled in the old city, thronged as it was with people of every sex, race and age, noisy and confident in their superior origin, trading in all kinds of weird and wonderful merchandise – some of it stolen and offered at eminently reasonable prices, to say the least.

Most brothels in Zurich (such premises do exist), are located in the old city, and as in any profitable and self-respecting business, each brothel individually advertises its wares, in the most direct, unmediated and tangible way possible: an impressive display of colour photographs showing the goods up for sale, in every imaginable posture.

As we often had occasion to cross the old city, we felt a certain sense of unease, confronted by the shop windows of the spacious houses of ill repute, until my wife took the initiative and suggested:

"Look at all the flesh on show here!"

I refused.

"Why?" she asked.

"I'm not interested."

"Take a look first, and then decide if you're interested or not."

"I'm not interested."

"I can sense the curiosity that you're charged up with."

We stopped in front of the display window of one of the more respectable whorehouses. My wife asked me to choose something. I refused.

"It can't do any harm," she insisted, "it's not as if you're going in there. Just tell me which girl and which pose appeal to you."

I refused again. And it was obvious I was going to keep on refusing, if necessary, from here to Alaska. And since, under pressure from my wife, I glanced in passing at the lurid display, it can be stated with confidence – there isn't the faintest hint of anything authentically Swiss there, taking its honoured place among the artistic creations of Swiss artists and displayed in impressive nude sculptures, at the corners and in the gardens of the city. Perhaps it's to the credit of the Swiss, or perhaps it's the reverse: the Swiss are fed up with Swiss people of the feminine gender and they chase after something, anything else to experience, so long as it isn't Swiss. One way or the other, you won't find in the shop windows of Zurich's brothels anything reminiscent of the buxom feminine form that is archetypically Swiss.

Every Saturday we visited the colourful flea-market and bought items for which, in the final analysis, there was no demand in our own country.

We weren't bored, we appreciated everything, and always promised ourselves we would return next year, a promise which we have kept in the letter and in the spirit, for more than a whole decade. We felt at home in Zurich. We enjoyed everything, and especially the pure air, clear of smog, redolent of fragrant groves. Anyway, this year was a departure from the familiar, agreeable and appropriate routine. One way or the other, a few days of relaxation made their invigorating contribution, until that Tuesday when the telephone once again ripped apart the smog-free air with typically Swiss brusqueness, and my wife and I knew that our serenity was about to be broken. Shmulik was on the line and he gave me a stark warning, one of the starkest imaginable.

"Beware," he said, "especially of anyone walking behind you. If this situation arises, do everything you can to shake him off, as quickly and effectively as possible. If there's no other choice, just run away from him, go into a shop, a cinema, a café, so you can come out again and disappear. I don't need to teach you these things, which I'm sure you learned in the 'Combat Squads' in Bulgaria. Anyway, always try to be part of a crowd. Warn your wife too.

Women, despite a tendency towards hysteria, have a more highly developed instinct than men have for detecting danger. My best wishes and my compliments to her. I hope there'll be no more need for phone conversations like this, before you come back to this country. Enjoy your vacation! Incidentally," Shmulik remembered – "checks in the blood-banks of several hospitals have yielded surprising results, and a number of cleaning workers and nurses, male and female, have been sacked, after confessing what was on their consciences. There was a network, not so much surprising as astounding. It's in our hands now. Stocks of blood are being held under rigorous supervision. You deserve a medal for this, but as you know, our country doesn't do medals. My best wishes again and see you soon!" End of conversation.

I told my wife, who characteristically became very tense. We went out for a walk in the woods, which in a sense was the longest living of all our walks, having been part of our routine for the past ten years.

Without realising it, my wife – despite her highly developed instinct for danger, as Shmulik had put it, and I – despite the exercises of more than thirty years ago and my experience, albeit ephemeral, of these things, were constantly turning our heads, checking every shadow, moving or otherwise, and sighing with relief when the pedestrian passed us by, taking no notice of us and making no impression on us whatsoever. This was the way we liked it.

Meetings with Israelis aren't uncommon. Especially around Jewish festival days, almost every fourth tourist arriving at the Bahnhoff is an Israeli. I went with my wife to the "H&M" clothing superstore; she picked up an item and went into one of the changing cubicles to try it on. At that moment I was approached by a tall woman with sunburnt face, flushed as if she had just run a marathon:

"Oh, it's you!" she began in Hebrew, which could not be described as anything but 'strident', and immediately added – "I recognised you! Speak Hebrew?" she went on to ask in English, not giving me a chance to reply, "I recognised her too!" She pointed to the cubicle where my wife had disappeared behind the curtain, passed a hand over her scalp, indicating that my wife's short hair was an unmistakable mark of recognition, and in the same emphatic tone she added, "I'm listening to her song all the time!"

"Which one?" I asked.

"All of them. All the discs, all on auto-play, I've got her on continuous loop!"

A mannish, formidable Israeli woman, and there's no wonder that I felt cowed by her solid presence. Suddenly she disappeared, as abruptly as she had descended on us, to my relief and to the relief of my wife, who had apparently heard every word she said from behind the curtain.

That's the way we are, we Israelis, and I only wish I could add "And it's nothing to be ashamed of".

We entered the "Manor", with the express intention of using the toilets on the top floor. As we climbed the stairs, my wife stopped beside a wooden wall panel covered with socks, of all materials, styles and sizes. She swooped on them with me following close behind, examined some of them, picked out nine pairs, and smiled one of her most charming smiles, pointing with her free right hand to the bundle clutched in her left and explained:

"Exactly the fabric I was looking for. Top quality, there's nothing like this at home." She went to the cash-desk, pulled out a credit card. While she waited for the conclusion of the paying process, her eye strayed over an extensive display of shoulder-bags, including an interesting specimen coloured khaki.

"This will go perfectly with the khaki skirt that we bought," she pointed out.

"A singular khaki shoulder-bag for the khaki skirt that we bought," I commented.

She picked up the bag, shouldered it, paced to right and left in front of the mirror and concluded: "It's a perfect match."

"And what about the bag you already have?"

— my voice wasn't hoarse, rather it was surprisingly clear.

"It's falling to bits," she declared, moving towards the cash-desk. Halfway there, she stopped, turned, came to me and urged me in a tone of entreaty, "Please, say 'yes' as if you meant it. Otherwise I won't feel comfortable buying this wonderful shoulder-bag, which is really cheap..."

"In francs," I commented.

"Over here," she replied, "francs are worth the same as shekels. If you don't want it, I'll do without it."

Of course I wanted it, contrary to all the principles of logic ingrained in my heart. But the day was fine, and without the bag it was sure to cloud over and something of the Japanese "wa" would go to waste.

We reached the toilets on the top floor, laden with socks and the bag, and as it turned out, they didn't impede us at all.

We went down from the toilets, not using the escalator but the lift that happened to be available. By mistake, we arrived on the basement floor. As we emerged from the belly of the lift, my wife's expert eye lighted on a khaki waistcoat, for men. She made a beeline for the waistcoat, as if all this had been planned a week ago, took it down from the peg, handed it to me and said:

"Put it on! No obligation to buy," she added.

The logic worked, the fitting room was close by; I put the waistcoat on.

"Nice work," I declared, glancing in the mirror and feeling quite comfortable in the garment. In the final analysis it's as my wife said: francs abroad are the same as shekels at home. Nevertheless, I tried to raise to the surface the ideologies of former times, regarding the petty bourgeoisie and the proletariat, the hunger afflicting the Dark Continent and the man who doesn't care, thinking only of wearing elegant waistcoats, and so on and so on. My wife was on her way to the cash-desk, the waistcoat over her left arm and the credit card in her right hand. I caught up with her by the cash-desk.

The charming young cashier was emitting lavish blessings. The credit card was proffered. I turned to my wife, with a vehement request:

"Tell the cashier they should be paying you a percentage..."

"How do I say that?"

"In English, of course."

She did as I asked.

The cashier listened attentively, and it turned out that unlike thousands of cashiers all over the world, she did not become a computer. Her unequivocal answer was evidence of a healthy sense of humour.

"Tell your husband," she said to my wife, "that he has a wonderful wife who buys him wonderful presents!"

Indeed, the charming cashier was absolutely right. My wife looked at her face and then at mine and burst into laughter, pure, sincere and captivating. I laughed with her and the cashier joined in. We left the "Manor".

CHAPTER TWELVE

The time was exactly 11.00 a.m. when the telephone ripped through our tranquillity with a sharp, dry and insistent ring.

My wife picked up the receiver. I stood facing her, watching the drastic changes affecting her face, which suddenly turned pale, a clear, unnatural pallor, such as I hadn't seen before then. Her hand gripping the receiver shook, once and then once more. The expression on her face was suddenly that of a small animal, closely pursued by a predator. I waited for the end of the conversation and eventually it came. The receiver was replaced on the cradle with a weary, ponderous movement, as if it weighed half a ton.

"What's up?" I asked, troubled to the last fibre of my nervous system, still in full working order.

"Someone has been asking about you, he wants you to go down to meet him, to discuss something important and extremely urgent. The reception clerk says the man looks suspicious to her. Apparently an Arab – according to her guess and judging by the name she read in his passport: Abd Rahman. She reckons the best thing to do is tell him you're not in your room, or you don't want to see him..."

Well, this was it, this was what Shmulik warned me about. In the "Combat Squads" we had learned that when you go out to meet an enemy, you should make sure you have equality of forces, carry a gun in your pocket at least. Of course, the best advice was to try to occupy a position of decisively superior strength.

"It seems to me, the best thing," – my wife commented, sensing my indecision, "is to accept the clerk's advice. She sounded scared out of her wits..."

"She's as nervous as a baby mouse!" I said without thinking.

"I hope you're not intending to go down there!"

"That is the most appropriate thing to do!" I declared provocatively, "After all, no one's going to dare to kidnap me or attack me in front of witnesses." I opened a counter-offensive, relying on the axiom that the best form of defence is attack. "The detective novels you read and the suspense films you watch, have broken down all the barriers of logic in your muddled mind."

My wife was silent for a long moment.

It was easy to guess at the struggle going on

in her heart, everything revolving around the question, how to stop me going down to the hotel reception, where the fragile clerk was sitting, scared to death; this was actually a good reason for not panicking, because if a kidnapper or hired assassin came, he would make a point of presenting a reassuring appearance, and on no account would he arouse fear or draw any kind of attention, thus jeopardising his project.

I decided to go down although I realised that my decision was based, in part, on a childish need to prove myself, to reassure my wife and perhaps to teach her, for future reference, that no purpose is ever served by panic and hysteria. I put on heavy boots, bearing in mind that if fisticuffs should ensue, any kick from a boot such as this, designed for climbing in the Alps, would put a leg in plaster for an appreciable time.

"I'll be right back!" I announced with a smile, intended to express unshakable confidence in the cultural tradition of the world, and to put firmly in their place all the action and suspense programmes which cram the television screens to the point of suffocation.

My wife tried to convince me that if she were to accompany me, the meeting would take on the cachet of official family business, and this would have a profoundly calming effect.

"I don't think there's going to be any need for that kind of calming," I commented, "and you would just be adding to the tension and unease. When all's said and done, look at the name my visitor has chosen for himself: 'Rahman', i.e. 'merciful'. It's a name that speaks for itself."

I bolstered my wife's faltering spirits with reassurances and expressions of confidence, and left the room. I went down in the lift, then along a narrow, dimly-lit corridor to the hotel reception. Behind the desk stood the young duty clerk, and when she saw me she nearly fainted. I looked around. In one of the armchairs sat a man, whose appearance immediately explained the reception clerk's unconventional behaviour.

The face was long, but not over-long and not narrow – in fact, long, broad and swarthy, scored by two deep grooves, with a crease in the cheek that was scorched by the desert sun. The eyes blazed. This was a Bedou with a lot of self-confidence, as if located in his natural environment – the desert. My quick glance unnerved him for a split-second. The first sentence that sprang into my mind, clear and acute, was: "He's done this before." He has already committed murder, and there's no reason for him to sitting here other than for purposes of murder. And the only logical conclusion to be drawn from this, the simple, numbing and inevitable conclusion, is that *he's here to murder me*. In my efforts to keep control of myself, I was alert to every one of my movements. I felt confidence and absence of fear, to a degree that could be considered unnatural. There was logic in this and a kind of assurance, capable of convincing one Abd Rahman, who had just arisen from the depths of Hell.

The situation reminded me of an incident from the distant past. On behalf of the "Combat Groups", I was given the task, along with Georgi, a rustic lad and former partisan, of following a certain suspect as closely as was possible, and finally, arresting him and taking him in for interrogation at the nearest militia headquarters. So we trailed along behind the "subject" who – so it seemed – paid us no attention, and made no attempt whatsoever to shake us off. The surveillance began at about nine in the evening. At ten-fifteen the "subject" went into a tavern and came out a few moments later. We resumed our pursuit. The "subject" arrived at an isolated house in the outskirts of the town. He knocked on a heavy, rough-hewn door, three knocks carefully spaced out, obviously a pre-arranged signal. The door opened and the "subject" disappeared behind it. The house also had a narrow window, neglected and dirty. Georgi assigned me to watch this while he guarded the door and the plan was, if anything happened, I was to cover him. The cool, late-autumn night began to oppress our over-tired bodies. We stood there from about ten-thirty until two in the morning. Then the door opened with an indignant creak and the "subject" came out. Without a moment's hesitation, Georgi approached the subject, showed him his ID card and told him to put his hands on the battered peaked-cap that he wore on his head. The "subject" did as he was told. He raised his left hand and laid the palm on his battered cap; his right hand however travelled down the cheaply tailored overcoat as far as the pocket, pulled out a bottle and brandished it in the air, with the obvious intention of bringing it down on Georgi's head.

At that very moment Georgi drew his pistol. The expression on his face immediately put that same sentence into my mind: "He's done this before" – he knows what it is to shoot a man at a range of half a metre, or point-blank. Sure enough a gunshot was heard, which later I was to describe as the shot of a marksman. The bullet hit the brandished bottle, smashing it to pieces, and the liquid it contained spilled over the arm of the one who had been waving it, exuding a strong smell of concentrated alcohol. The man was stunned. His first, instinctive and unexpected reaction was to kneel at Georgi's feet, with an outburst of hysterical weeping, accompanied by belches.

Later we discovered that the man with the bottle wasn't the sinister envoy of western Anglo-American imperialist reactionaries, intent on subverting the firm foundations of the enlightened socialist regime in Bulgaria, but just someone who kept a mistress in that isolated house. When visiting his mistress, he had not forgotten to stop at that tavern on the way and buy strong liquor, and with typical and depressing Bulgarian thrift, as the bottle hadn't been emptied, he was taking the remainder for himself. He had come under suspicion after missing three of the obligatory weekly meetings, which all supporters of the regime were supposed to attend, and when he was not found at home, the process was set in motion. It can well be imagined how astounded the man must have been by what awaited him outside, on leaving the house of his mistress.

Mr Rahman, sitting there in the armchair in the hotel lobby, he too had certainly done this before.

I turned to the clerk. And then a shot was heard, ringing in my ears and deafening them completely, all at once and for a long time to come, and seeming to set the hotel reeling, quiet as it was at this hour of the day. Quickly I moved probing hands over my body. I wasn't injured. I turned to look at Mr Rahman and was struck dumb with amazement. Mr Rahman had fallen from his armchair, hitting his head hard against the parquet floor of the lobby. A spreading bloodstain, surrounding his scalp like a halo, testified that he had been shot in the head.

Without a moment's delay, the fragile clerk alerted the police, who rapidly appeared on the scene with all the noisy paraphernalia that is inevitable in cases such as these: Hollywood-style sirens of police vehicles and speeding ambulance. The police had to cope with the hotel guests, who had come downstairs on hearing the gunshot which had brought their quiet routine to such an abrupt end. Among them was my wife, who managed to utter an authentically Israeli crisis-call, its content indefinable. She was soon to be relieved and satisfied, seeing me healthy and whole.

The cops were gathering statements and they asked me to come in for questioning, immediately if possible. I reassured my wife and rode with her in the spacious and comfortable police car, no siren blaring this time. The ambulance crew loaded Abd Rahman, or rather his corpse, in their vehicle and whisked him away to the pathology lab.

I sat down facing a young and energetic investigating officer who asked questions that were pertinent, although awfully standard. Country of origin? Was this the first time I had been a guest in the hotel?

"The eleventh time"

"How often?"

"Every year."

"Enemies – at home or here?"

"None that I know of."

"Did you see who shot Mr Abd Rahman?"

"No," I replied with a deep and emphatic sigh of relief and admitted I was curious myself to know this; after all, as the clerk had reported, it was me that Mr Rahman wanted to see.

"That's what complicates everything," the young officer declared with obvious unease.

Here I saw fit to diffuse the tense atmosphere by translating the assassin's name for the officer's benefit:

"The name Abd Rahman," I explained, "means servant of God who is full of mercy." The cop digested this, impressed:

"What weird names these people have," he commented – to demonstrate his lack of concern, also his appreciation of someone who understands such a complicated language as Arabic and last but not least, to prove himself a man with a sense of humour, something not typical of cops in general and of Swiss ones in particular.

"If," the officer added, "we knew that someone was tailing Mr Rahman, and got his shot in first, we'd be wiser. We found a heavy revolver in Mr Rahman's pocket, loaded, of Swiss manufacture," he saw fit to inform me.

"In other words – he bought the gun in Switzerland?" I asked innocently.

The officer nodded.

"Do we know where from?" – more affected innocence.

"From a shop," the young man replied with engaging simplicity.

"So anyone who wants, can buy a heavy Swiss revolver – just from a shop?"

"If he pays the price for it," the cop nodded, "and gives proof of identity and has a good reason for wanting it."

I didn't ask any more questions.

"Anyway, the mystery man who tailed Mr Rahman saved your life. Take care, Sir," he saw fit to warn me, with an earnest expression on his young face – "you won't always have such an efficient guardian angel on hand!"

"Many thanks," – I thanked him and thanked him again, "If you catch the shooter, please pass on my deep and sincere appreciation and the gratitude of my family."

"I promise we'll do that," the young cop smiled, standing and holding out a fleshy, heavy and cold hand. He shook my hand and my wife's, warmly and sincerely, and added: "You have good reason to celebrate. Champagne would seem to fit the occasion – unless you have some objection to alcohol."

"To champagne, never! Can we invite you to join us for a glass?"

"Thanks very much. I'm addicted to champagne, but not just now."

CHAPTER THIRTEEN

The young police officer phoned. In his opinion and on the basis of his professional judgment, it was most advisable that I should have a professional bodyguard, at least until the end of my holiday. He recommended to me a young man who was experienced, loyal and conscientious, named Karl. Karl would come to the hotel this afternoon, and he hoped I would appreciate the exceptional efforts he was making to guarantee my safety and security, and not reject his services.

He concluded with all kinds of salutations and promises, waited about half a minute for my response and when none came, wished me a good afternoon and cut the connection, with all the delicacy appropriate to a police officer.

Karl was a youth of about seventeen-eighteen. Thin and wiry, muscular, with an intelligent look about him. He offered his services "pursuant to a conversation with the police commander", for the same fee that he charged everyone: one hundred francs per day. I hesitated. It didn't seem to me his services were vital. I felt a certain affection towards him, the affection of a grandfather towards his grandson, but nothing more. Was it worth paying a hundred francs a day for this? I didn't turn him down out of hand. I said, I would weigh up his offer. At first sight he seemed suitable, but there were other factors to be considered. At this point young Karl tried to meet me halfway:

"I'm not allowed to reduce the fee. What I can promise, is to do a reliable job whichever days I'm guarding you. You can be secure in the knowledge that no one will dare get too close to you." We parted with a firm handshake. About an hour later, there was a call from the hotel reception. A girl called Irena was looking for me, to discuss something of importance to both of us. I announced that I would be coming down within a quarter of an hour at the most, if Madame Irena was prepared to wait. The immediate answer was: she was prepared.

"Take care you don't get tangled up in anything," my wife advised.

I went down to reception. Waiting there was a pretty young Swiss, by which I mean a girl overflowing with youth, energy and health and something more, that could be defined as integrity, since her body was the lithe body of a woman, with nothing wasted about it.

Everything was in its place, having the right shape and the precise, classical proportions. Making her acquaintance was easy. We went down to the café. I ordered herbal tea, she – a glass of mineral water.

"Awfully sorry to be bothering you," Irena began with an apology in English that was colloquial and at the same time, vehement in tone. She went on to explain that she was Karl's girlfreind. "I may as well come straight to the point and tell you, that if you agree to employ him, and this is something that's very important to him, and in a moment I'll explain why, I'll be happy to pay half of the cost. Karl is a very talented lad. His grandfather was the most senior police officer not only in Zurich, but in the whole canton of Zurich. In other words: his grandfather was the Zurich police chief. Highly respected, a man of knowledge and experience, quick on the uptake. He was killed in the line of duty! (The last sentence was spoken with emphatic tribal pride.) Karl's father was a senior police officer in Zurich too. Karl thought he'd be taken on in the Zurich force and he'd make his career there, more or less automatically. For some reason, up until now he hasn't been accepted. I don't want to go too deeply into things, because these are really family matters and it doesn't seem right to involve strangers in them... Friends and relatives are worried about Karl and from time to time they throw him a little bone and this makes Karl happy, ridiculously happy. Karl," she went on to say with a bitter kind of smile, "has a personality completely different from the personalities of his ancestors. He's enthusiastic, impulsive sometimes, with the vision of a poet, not always capable of behaving in a rational manner, and those are the traits in him that I'm madly in love with, but they trip him up all the time. All the same, he's determined to be a cop and he's not giving up on it, and I'm sure that you, Sir, will appreciate his unconditional loyalty, his tireless devotion to duty, in all circumstances. Karl's happiness is so important to me."

"Why is that?" I asked, and at that moment I seemed to myself to be identifying with the stolidity of outlook that is supposedly typically Germanic.

"Because I love him! I know it's a cliché, but he's the one and only love of my heart!"

I was silent for a moment, as was she.

"Tell him he can start from tomorrow."

"He'll think that's suspicious, I'm sure you understand, Sir. I don't want him to know anything about this meeting we're having, not even the slightest hint."

"I'll tell him myself."

"You've made my day, and my week, maybe more."

I phoned Karl. Next day, he began trailing around after me, with dedication surpassing the proverbial dedication of Saint Bernard dogs.

My wife sensed, and commented on the fact, that the amiable Swiss boy was shadowing us tirelessly. Next Saturday we visited the flea market. Karl, who was supposed to be seeing but unseen, certainly kept a keen eye on anyone coming close to us, but he was also clearly visible to anyone who wanted to see him. And so it happened, that at about two in the afternoon, there was a commotion behind us. Blows were exchanged, and the police were called. Karl was arrested along with a swarthy individual, a man with a long moustache, who later turned out to be a peace-loving visitor from Qatar, who made the mistake that day of wearing his traditional national costume, thereby arousing the suspicions of Karl, who did not hesitate to knock him to the ground with a few well-aimed punches, and to check out his body with lightning speed, in search of concealed weapons, which weren't there. We met the next day. He was very sorry about the trouble he had caused, unintentionally. We both realised that the connection between us was at an end. I paid him what I owed him, and later I refused to accept Irena's contribution. I wished her a brilliant marriage. We were unanimous in believing Karl was a youth of outstanding qualities, and she was lucky to have him. The police officer apologised and promised, without being asked, to find some other way of keeping an eye on us.

Every morning we used to go up to the top floor of the "Co-op" store located in "Saint Annahoff", to drink decaffeinated cappuccino and plan the day ahead. We found a table under a huge, curtained window; the area covered by the curtain could be widened or reduced by turning handles. We liked this table, especially because of the two-seater bench which we found very comfortable. Like us and not far from us – every morning an older couple used to sit, and almost in the centre of the room was a woman in early middle-age who said she was American, and had apparently been sent to Switzerland for psychiatric treatment. Sometimes we exchanged greetings, sometimes not. The café was pleasant, the cappuccino excellent, to my wife's taste as well, and the place served as a good starting point for a day of leisure in Zurich, and for the objectives we had set ourselves. And this morning, the American woman took out a camera and aimed it at us. The trauma of Abd Rahman and of the shooting was still very fresh, the wound still open. I had heard of "cameras" that fired bullets at the objects they were aimed at.

"No!" I protested vehemently, remembering the warnings of Shmulik and the young police officer, and the lessons learned from my own experience. She paused for a moment, and then asked my wife:

"Why is he objecting?"

"He has reasons of his own, but" – my wife pointed out, "it is normal to ask permission before taking someone's picture." The lady turned to me:

"May I take a picture of the two of you?" The voice was gentle, thoroughly amiable. I answered in a tone of offended dignity:

"I'd much rather you didn't."

The middle-aged couple turned to stare at me with a pair of question-marks, which soured the atmosphere completely.

A more modest question mark was posed by my wife, who lost no time, turned to the American lady and asked in her fluent English:

"Why do you want to take our picture?"

The woman softened:

"I'm going home and I want to preserve some memories. You and your husband are among the more pleasant ones. Does your husband find me intolerable?"

"Heaven forbid!" my wife exclaimed, putting the treatment before the injury. The woman was quick to draw her conclusions:

"Then he likes me?" – her hard features glowed, with something like infinite satisfaction, curing all ills, psychological ones too. My wife suddenly found herself straying into a minefield. A rapid retreat seemed the logical solution in these circumstances.

"Yes, he likes you."

"So why does he object to me taking his picture and keeping it as a souvenir?"

My wife said the first thing that came into her head, which was in fact what she believed to be the truth:

"He lived for many years under a communist regime and as you know, everyone there suffers to some degree from chronic paranoia."

Any reaction on the part of the ailing American lady could have been expected, even a violent assault on my wife or on me or on both of us. But it seemed that the Swiss were treating her condition with their typical dedication and expertise.

"Yes," the American lady agreed without hesitation, "Joe Stalin was paranoid too."

"That's right," my wife backed her up with excessive warmth and added by way of emphasis: "No one comes out from under a communist regime without a touch of paranoia in his heart."

Later, she admitted to me that she was telling the truth as she had experienced it and that she had been rather surprised by my reaction, exceeding any logical boundaries, and added: "It's true that we have to be careful after the incident with Mr Abd Rahman, but here everything is calm... We've known those people for more than a month now and they've known us."

"All the same," I retorted, "you have no conception of the other reality."

"You mean the communist reality?"

I had no option but to confirm this. The atmosphere had been spoiled, and we agreed that it was time to leave the café.

The next day we happened to be in the area. I asked my wife to wait for me while I went to the familiar toilets.

"Take care, don't let the American lady see you!"

"No need to worry!" I assured her. The moving staircase carried me up four floors to the familiar café. I stood in the doorway and glanced briefly at our regular table – with the two-seater bench. A corpulent, middle-aged American man was sitting there. The "American lady" moved across, stood behind him, and with undisguised anger, began pulling back curtains and opening windows. Wind and sun flooded in, swamping the American who tried in vain to compress his big body. I turned to the toilets. On the way out I met the large American, who scanned me with a suspicious look, and asked:

"Are you Swiss, sir?"

"No."

"Tourist?"

"Yes."

"Me too. These Swiss guys – weird or what?"

"I don't think so," I gave my honest opinion.

"I just sat down for a few minutes in this

café" – he pointed with his heavy chin at "our" seat, now deserted. "Some lady comes along, don't know if she's quite sane or not, tries every which way she can to make me move. I asked her – why? She said – you're taking the place of a charming couple who may be arriving here soon. Isn't that crazy?" the American asked in a self-righteous voice.

"Crazy," I agreed, and hurriedly took my leave of him, running to the downward escalator.

My wife responded to the story:

"Poor woman! She's going to be keeping our place for us for days to come. She'll be so disappointed! Let's hope it doesn't interfere with her psychiatric treatment – you and your communist paranoia!"

I shared this hope.

CHAPTER FOURTEEN

We sat in our spacious, familiar room, and didn't switch on the television.

"Interested?" I asked and handed her the remote control.

"Not at all. I prefer the quiet, the sights, the rain falling calmly, mercifully I would say." And then she added: "The weather forecasts have got it completely wrong."

"Not completely," I commented.

"It seems, the weather forecasters aren't doing their job properly. Or perhaps," she added, "this profession isn't an exact science."

"A science, yes, and exact – yes, but all the same, it depends on who is doing it"

"What's that supposed to mean?" my wife asked, her curiosity aroused, "What are you referring to?"

"Getting the job done is what counts. In other words" – I gave the answer in advance to the question, or perhaps, a flood of questions, "they aren't doing a conscientious job."

"What is a conscientious job?"

"A job done by someone who loves it and is a believer."

"That sounds a bit idealistic," she commented, with some justification.

"A story occurs to me," I countered, "about professions and the way they are practised. It's a story that's all true, and it's from an Arab source."

"I'm all ears."

"In fact," I said, "I heard it from Amin Abu Halil, one fine evening in New York City. We were sitting in my room, going through material that he was going to be tested on, and the subject of choosing professions came up. Amin claimed that according to the ancient Arab perception, still valid today, a man is predestined to a certain profession, even if he thinks it's his own choice. In fact, God guides him towards it. And this is the story that Amin told me.

"In the Muslim world, a few decades ago, pilgrims to Mecca complained to the sovereign, King Ibn Saud, about a small Muslim tribe, living in the mountains, all of whose members practised a single trade, exclusively, handed down from father to son and grandson and great grandson, for centuries. And the trade, on which this small mountain tribe subsisted – was plunder.

"King Ibn Saud sent a high-powered delegation to talk to the dignitaries of the tribe and demand that they abandon their ancient profession, and stop harassing decent Muslims in their efforts to uphold the commandment of Hajj, supreme among commandments.

"The dignitaries of the tribe listened attentively to the eminent delegation, considered what they had to say, and gave an unequivocal answer:

For as long as the tribe has existed, it has made its living from robbing pilgrims, a profession enjoined upon us by Allah, and we know no other trade. Nor have we any intention of learning another trade and dishonouring the tradition of our forefathers. We regret this defiance of His Majesty the King.

"Ibn Saud, 'His Majesty' was enraged. He sent an even more high-powered delegation, with a categorical command to pass on:

This plunder is to be stopped immediately and at any price. I shall not tolerate any such profession in my kingdom, a profession that derives not from Allah but the laziness of mankind, those who are weak in mind and in body and under the influence of Satan. If I hear of any further acts of pillage against holy pilgrims, I shall not leave a remnant or a relic of this rebellious tribe, I shall exterminate and destroy and leave no trace of it on God's holy earth and under His clear skies. This is my command, given to you by divine right.

"This time, the small tribe made no reply at all to the distinguished delegation, for better or worse. And in fact, Ibn Saud displayed exemplary patience, until the next Hajj, when a column of pilgrims was attacked and robbed by the practitioners of that ancient profession. He mustered his soldiers and led them down to the sea, where they all bathed, put on their warlike headgear, took up their ancient swords, and prayed. And King Ibn Saud addressed his troops, and made them swear to destroy and exterminate every living thing in that tribal encampment, whether man or beast, and burn the encampment and let no one evade the avenging sword of God, and obliterate the memory of this rebellious tribe, from the face of the holy earth and from under the clear skies of God. And as he said, so it was. The well-drilled army attacked with their ancient curved swords, set alight everything that would burn and slaughtered, over one whole day, all that belonged to that rebellious tribe, man and beast, people irrespective of age and sex."

I admitted this was an interesting story.

"And it's all true. No Scheherazade here! " Amin assured me.

CHAPTER FIFTEEN

We caught colds. With everything that goes with catching cold – especially abroad. Pains in the joints, difficulty breathing, runny noses, coughing, low temperature, using tissues by the ton and a strong desire to go home. A sense of home, powerful and radical, incomparable, unambiguous certitude that it exists. Or as my wife, with the deepest roots in the homeland, summed it up: "Abroad has exhausted itself!"

In my youth, in my schooldays, my classmates made persistent efforts to make me aware I was a foreigner. The country, which I, like them, called my country, was not my country in any sense whatsoever, in any way at all. I argued. I claimed that both my grandfathers fought to liberate our country from Turkish rule, I said "our country" in a faltering voice, because I knew I couldn't hope to convince my classmates, not under any circumstances, not at all. And all the patriotic songs, giving wings to the young spirit, which we sang in class with youthful, irresistible enthusiasm, did not apply to me. They applied to all the others, not me. Because I wasn't a son of the land that I called my country. I was an alien plant. More than that – I wasn't wanted. From one eternity to the next. My new homeland I didn't love. But it was the only homeland offered to me. I needed a homeland as a child needs a supportive, affectionate mother, loving or not.

Catching a cold wasn't the reason behind the primeval sacred longings – honest, powerful, revered, sincere. Rather it was the age-old pain of the orphan, forever a fugitive, the acute self-awareness, growing more intense, consuming every part – good or bad, sincerity that nothing can resist, the truth that you have a homeland and you're prepared to sacrifice everything for it – however pathetic this may be, theatrical and staged – and there's nothing to compare with it. And this is what my wife declared as a natural, self-evident conclusion: "Abroad has exhausted itself!" And it wasn't the illness, which of course we had to contend with, the first priority being to find a suitable answer for my wife, a concise answer to her question: "What is illness?"

The answer:

In the Middle Ages, they called man a "microcosm"; i.e. a miniaturised copy of the world, which exists by virtue of preservation of divine justice and the balance of natural forces – and as it has turned out, they were absolutely right. "Progress" and "culture", which try to make out of every object and every topic something synthetic, have ignored some important issues, opposing the excess of arrogance that suffuses them.

"The person who dispels God from his presence, and he is the average person today, lives on his senses. Believing only in the senses, devoted to the senses and dying by them. You could say, man tries to derive sensual pleasure from everything."

"Like for example?" she interjected.

"Like for example, eating not because you're hungry and you need nourishment, but as often as possible, for the pleasure of the palate alone – and the result is?" I addressed the question to my audience and she was not slow to answer:

"Sickness."

"And when one tries to make sexual indulgence a principle of life, the result is?"

"AIDS."

"That's the modern outcome. Alongside AIDS march those famous war heroes – syphilis, gonorrhoea, and in recent times, chlamydia trachomatis and herpes. And no doubt, sexual promiscuity will have further surprises in store for us. And finally, at the moment, pain-killing drugs such as morphine, cocaine and similar substances, are turning into sources of sensual pleasure, with results that are known only too well. And in case I haven't told you this before, in the fifties I knew a doctor called Serr, a Jew of Polish origin, sent by the Germans to the death-camps. He told me, and later he published an article about it in a prestigious medical journal, that in one of the camps he found some of his former patients, including cases of acute heart disease, cancer and diabetes. He examined them again after several months spent in the extermination camp, and could find no symptoms of those serious medical conditions. He reported on this to the German doctor who was his superior, and the latter, genius that he was, ordered the execution of those patients, although they had been cured, by the lethal hunger and other privations suffered in the camp, of diseases that were reckoned incurable."

"German genius indeed," my wife concurred. "What's to be done?" she demanded to know.

"From everything you have heard, what is the conclusion?"

"Not to over-indulge."

"Bull's-eye!" I declared. "In all senses, in all sectors."

"And in the meantime, what are we going to do about the illness we're suffering from?"

"We must methodically probe the crevices of

our consciousness, bring out and replay the fantasies we've entertained recently, the plans we've made for the future, the visible things and the invisible, and when we find the black sheep, we'll expel them with courage and without compromise, a total expulsion."

A few days passed. One morning we both rose and found, that of all the pains, in all parts of the body, of all the appeals for mercy – no trace was left. And then my wife put a question that she had been keeping for a suitable time, and the time was now:

"What about all those invisible creatures?" she asked, and added by way of clarification, "Microbes, viruses?"

"If body and mind are in balance," I answered her calmly, "they can come to terms with them, just as an efficient housewife comes to terms with the dirt in her house. She has vacuum cleaners and other instruments available to her and her home is always clean and sparkling, like yours in fact."

"So it's good to be a housewife."

"It's excellent to be a housewife, if that is what you really want to be. If you're a housewife and you don't want to be a housewife, it will make you ill, and your family too."

And although I am opposed, totally opposed, to anything betraying the slightest hint of preaching, and what I have just finished writing gives off a distinct and more or less tolerable whiff of childish sermonising, and you, my reader, are no doubt proud of your intellectual atheism – try all the same to retain in your memory what you have just read. I hope you don't need it, and if it turns out that you do need it, don't be ashamed to make the necessary use of it. You have nothing to lose, except a morsel of pride which is of no real value at all, and may you and yours be well.

CHAPTER SIXTEEN

In the evening, the phone once again shattered the blessed silence of the room. My wife and I both ran to the phone. She got there first, and picked up the receiver with an air of triumph.

"Shmulik!" she announced, handing over to me.

"Ask him," she added as an afterthought, "to stop sending us all these demons from Hell."

I took the receiver.

"Please tell your wife," Shmulik responded, having evidently overheard her, "that we're not the ones sending you demons from Hell, these or any others." It seemed that Shmulik had been kept well-informed. Now he wanted to hear an account from first hand a "full account" as he put it. I complied willingly enough.

"Mr Abd Rahman came here to pay a courtesy call. His name means 'merciful' but he doesn't live up to it."

I told him everything. He uttered a grunt of satisfaction.

"The version you gave to the police inspector was very good," he concluded, "just make sure you stick to it all the way. It's possible they'll call you in for another interview. Sometimes, in democratic countries, the police are working under pressure from the government and from the public, who demand to know everything in detail, as precise as possible and the more sensational the better. Remember what you said and don't deviate from it to left or right. Until they realise they have no prospect of getting anything more out of you, even a fabricated or imaginary version. I'm having to watch what I say in this conversation too. It's very possible that interested parties, and there's no shortage of them, are eavesdropping on us at this moment, with all ears."

Later, when we met back at home, Shmulik told me more:

"Your assessment of Mr Rahman was quite correct. He had done this a number of times. And if you want to know, one of the passports he held was an Israeli one. He was a Bedou from this country, husband to five wives and father to more than thirty offspring, all of them supported out of national insurance. Recently he's earned millions from his special talent, shooting accurately over a considerable distance from any position required, however impossible it may be. He got a contract on you and set out to do the job. Our services took it on themselves to stop him, and they hired the good offices of Paul Atlas, Abd Rahman's sworn competitor. Mr Atlas went everywhere Mr Rahman went, even following him to the toilet if that was necessary. He went into your hotel and sat down not far from Mr Rahman, trying to find a suitable position, that wouldn't look suspicious and would give him the best prospect of taking him out in time, as it was obvious Rahman was determined to act, and soon. Paul Atlas wasn't favourably impressed by you. You struck him as physically weak and he said he wouldn't bet on you. Everything happened with unexpected speed and Mr Paul Atlas did a sterling job, at the right moment and in the right way, and earned 20,000 dollars, in ready cash, from his employers, one of whom was the one talking to you now. It occurs to me, that a suitable post at the Nes Ziona Biological Institute might appeal to you. One way or the other, we were all relieved with the way it worked out and I guess you were too, your wife as well. We've been drinking to your health," and he concluded this conversation with the vehement Biblical exhortation: "Be strong and bold!" I responded with a "Be strong and bold!" no less vehement than his.

The next day I was recalled to the police

station. They wanted to know about the phone conversation I had held yesterday – who was the other speaker, what was it about, and what were my connections with him. It seems one of the hotel employees had leaked to them the information about the call, and because the conversation had been in Hebrew, they were not much the wiser. With commendable composure I declared I wasn't prepared to answer these questions and I concluded – playing the slighted tourist – I wasn't obliged to either.

The business of upholding the law is something which the Swiss police evidently take very seriously. The officer turned to me and with plain and emphatic brusqueness he declared:

"You're not a fool. You know that when a top-ranking hitman is sent to take you out, there's nothing casual about it. I haven't a shadow of a doubt you know perfectly well why he came after you, and you know perfectly well it's my duty to get something logical out of you. Give me a line to follow, a line with something solid behind it, as to who wanted to eliminate you and why, and I'll leave you alone. You have my word as an officer. Around here, the word of an officer counts for a great deal more than any other kind of promise, oath or solemn vow. Help me Sir, and I can help you."

His request was sincere. I thought it over briefly, and I reckoned I'd found a way out:

"It has to do with the Arab-Israeli conflict.

As you know, Arabs are very quick to take offence, and when they're out for revenge they never give up."

"You impugned the honour of one of their top people?" – the officer clutched the straw that I held out to him.

I nodded in an unequivocal fashion. He hastily jotted down, in broad handwriting, clearly legible to the one sitting opposite him: "Arab-Israeli conflict. Revenge." We both breathed sighs of relief. He stood up and held out to me his broad and heavy hand, and parted from me with an endless series of felicitations, for a good day, a happy year and a nice life. And there was yet to be a further meeting between us. I was summoned urgently to the police station, the day after that interview.

"Help me to help you. You have to understand, your life is in danger" he pulled out a drawer, taking out a photograph of me standing at the window of my hotel room, shot with a telescopic lens. "You have to understand," continued the investigating officer, becoming more friendly by the moment – "these people are clever. This photo was found in Mr Rahman's pocket. People are watching you, there's no doubt about that. Give me details about yourself and I'll find them, keep tabs on them. And you will be protected as befits you, as befits every guest in the state of Switzerland, with its long tradition of neutrality."

My refusal was disappointing and absolute.

"In any case," he continued in an affable tone, intended to inspire confidence, "I'll put one of my people in the hotel. He'll keep an eye on you, and you won't know he's there. This is being done for your benefit." We parted with a hearty handshake – Swiss style. A handshake that isn't obligatory, isn't warm and yet at the same time – radiates friendship.

The next day I noticed a young man, very young in fact, a little on the plump side, in a shirt, trousers and jacket of standard police colours, without any identifying marks or insignia of rank. He followed me into the dining-room, and went out with me, until I disappeared into the lift. On the third day, my "escort" started eating with gusto in the dining-room, flirting with the waitresses and the chambermaids. I didn't mention it to my wife, hoping she wouldn't notice for herself, a hope that was quickly dashed.

"What kind of a cop is that?" she commented – indicating the plumpish figure who was sitting at a table not far from ours, wolfing down sausage, bacon and eggs and drinking coffee, following every shapely female tourist with a hungry look, and constantly trying out clumsy chat-up lines on the waitress who served his coffee, winking at her just as clumsily.

"It's no business of ours," I answered my

wife.

She took this in, digested it and commented in a whisper: "Anyone can tell he's a plain-clothes cop."

"Perhaps that's intentional," I replied equably, and the subject was dropped from the agenda. For a week the undercover cop ate and drank in the hotel, and socialised with the hotel staff of the feminine gender, and then he disappeared as if he had never been.

The budget of the Zurich municipality, it seemed, was not unlimited.

CHAPTER SEVENTEEN

Sunday came. One of those Sundays abroad, redolent of good will, relaxation and calm, upholding the ancient imperatives of the primeval act, the Sabbath Day, when God "rested", in other words – the act of creation came to the stage of completion and required a backward look, to enjoy what had been finished, the beauty and innocence and harmony and restrained power of the primeval world. Below the hotel the great lake sparkled; two boats made steady progress along it, moving in opposite directions. The heavens spoke blessings, the earth spoke peace, such that it seemed the hand of man could do nothing to impair it. We sprang from our beds, showered, went down to the dining-room and helped ourselves to a lavish breakfast, and without further discussion we dressed in clothing appropriate for a Sunday. My wife wore an olive-coloured sweater, and I, the waistcoat which we had bought not long before, its colour complementing the luxuriance of my wife's sweater, which spoke of activity and willingness to give. In the lift, my wife took a long look at our reflections in the full-length mirror installed there, and commented:

"Look at the harmony of colours. And all quite unplanned."

"External harmony reflects the internal," was my trite response, which nevertheless earned me a kiss. We went out to the wood that we knew so well, climbing the slope to the clearing at the top and moving further on, filling our quasi-desiccated Israeli lungs with great gulps of the invigorating, oxygen-rich air of abroad. The desire to sing was not repressed. We sang. Not at full volume, but without restraint. My wife didn't unleash the full power of the God-given gift residing in her throat – those vocal cords that it seemed incredible any mortal could be endowed with, perhaps with the intention of sparing me feelings of inferiority or perhaps the opposite – sparing me the temptation to swell with vicarious pride – or for a combination of both motives together, something not uncommon for complex types like us. I sang, or rather I joined in or accompanied her, keeping as low a profile as possible. And the song went on. At the first turning, a chamois stood facing us, looking perplexed. Not that he can have been much of a connoisseur of music; after all the whole business of vocal articulation must seem crazy to the race of the chamois. They aren't used to such phenomena, especially not the Swiss chamois. In fact this one recoiled from us, shying away and clearing our path.

"That's a good sign," my wife commented, referring to the appearance of the enchanting creature. "To be released from all the tension, if only for a moment!"

This *if only for a moment* was sincere and came from deep down.

"No need to exaggerate," I declared with typical cheeriness. She was offended.

"What exaggeration are you talking about?" she protested and added: "Someone's shooting at my husband, his life's in danger, and all our happiness, it seems, is hanging by a thread – and you're talking about exaggeration!"

"My mistake!" – I hurriedly grasped the reliable pillar of blessed domestic harmony and changed the subject: "Look how peaceful it is all around. We should breathe it deep into our lungs, our hearts, our whole being – while we can. For a year at least none of this is going to be available to us."

"So it seems," my wife was quick to respond. "Still, all the same, there is something in the air!.."

"The air is balmy, energising, spreading encouragement and happiness!"

"Now you're exaggerating!" she declared.

"It seems to me you caught it from me," I protested.

"Caught what?" she demanded to know.

"What you call 'Bulgarian pessimism'."

"Not at this moment!" she insisted.

"How is it possible that in this quiet, festal atmosphere of a Sunday, in the wood, where nothing is wrong, where a chamois comes to greet us, and he's the emissary of something sublime, unearthly, not of flesh and blood, and every tree is singing and we are singing along too – how can you find any reason to say *Still, all the same*?"

My wife recovered her composure: "You're right, I take it back," and there and then she launched into "Tipperary", an optimistic song in which all our affection was invested. We crossed a woodland clearing carpeted with dense, natural grass, trimmed not by the hand of man and smelling pungent. I sang at maximum volume, or rather, I meant to sing so loudly that the trees would shake on their foundations, but I didn't get the chance. At that moment, a strident, unsteady voice was heard, commanding:

"Halt!"

I turned round. A tall, thin man was pointing a heavy pistol at me from a range of less than five paces. He was clutching the shiny weapon in both hands, which shook and made the pistol shake. It was obvious there was no empathy between him and the gun. The two of us, the man holding the pistol and aiming it at me, and I, stood face to face, perplexed by the unnatural situation, supposedly forced upon both of us to the same catastrophic extent, which caused the one holding the gun to shake more erratically than ever. Perhaps a second passed, perhaps a minute. The gunman fired, I heard the whistle of the bullet (it wasn't the wind). A fraction of a second later, a burst of automatic fire was heard, and before I knew what was going on, I found myself lying on the fragrant grass, which seemed to smell poisonous to me, and I'd have preferred some other grassy pillow, enclosed, artificial, in a small but quiet garden, even a plastic lawn. What propelled me to the ground, was a strong and decisive hand, full of unexpected and irresistible strength, despite its diminutive, almost childlike size – the hand of my wife, who fell together with me on that pungent carpet, repellent in its luxuriance.

"What are you doing!" I protested, trying to give a human dimension to the picture.

"Putting into practice what I've read in the thrillers and seen in the mafia movies that you hate so much!"

I almost laughed aloud – how lucky I was to have this woman! – I told myself. A few more sporadic shots heralded the end of the show.

I seemed to hear the high-pitched whine emerging from the blank screen, telling me – *We've entertained you long enough, so please change the channel or turn off the set and go to sleep.*

Someone approached us with stealthy tread.

Without moving a limb, I took a sidelong glance. It was the investigating officer. He saw me looking at him and declared in his hideously accented English:

"You're still causing problems, to yourselves and to us. Go home, for everyone's sake and yours in particular. Or you'll go home in coffins. You can get up now!"

The last sentence sounded like an order. I got up slowly, held out a hand to my wife and pulled her to her feet. Her festive sweater, my waistcoat, were covered with tiny leaves, grains of dust and all kinds of mites. I brushed off quickly, as much as could be brushed off quickly, from my wife's sweater, before she could realise the state she was in – with consequent change of mood. I forgot, she takes her mood from the state of my clothing too.

We accompanied the young police officer, whose name turned out to be Heinrich Zimmerman. About five metres from the place that we fell, lay a tall, thin man, looking out of place in the Swiss landscape. Heinrich pointed at him with his angular chin, jutting forward like the prow of a ship in a storm:

"Olaf Olsen, holding a Norwegian passport, of mixed Norwegian-Swedish parentage." He pulled a handkerchief from the pocket of his tight trousers, picked up the pistol which lay impotently beside the corpse of Olaf Olsen, and I saw at close quarters the heavy "Zig Zauer" which a few moments before had been aimed at me. Later, I was told this is one of the best handguns in the world.

"Bought in a shop, I suppose," I commented in a mildly ironical tone, aimed at diffusing some of the tension.

"Hans!" Heinrich cried and from among the trees a broad-shouldered Swiss appeared, heavily built but unexpectedly agile and light on his feet. He took the pistol, wrapped in the handkerchief.

"Yes, in a shop," Heinrich confirmed, and it was obvious he was bursting with repressed feelings and feeling an irresistible need to pour everything out and tell all he knew. I encouraged him, as I was no less interested than he was in hearing what he had to say. And this was his story:

The Norwegian-Swedish gentleman arrived in Switzerland not long ago. He runs a toy-shop in Oslo... the shop is only a cover, and I must surely understand what he means. I understood but didn't respond. He continued his story as we walked, at a sedate and casual Swiss-style pace along the path leading back to the hotel. "The man was a sleeper," Heinrich felt the need to explain to us. People interested in shedding my blood, and they might just have a point – after Rahman went to a better world, they obviously weren't going to give up and they sent Olaf Olsen to Switzerland on a specific assignment, with the photograph of me and all the rest. The first thing Mr Olaf Olsen did was go to a gun-shop in Zurich. He asked for a handgun and before being asked what he wanted it for, told the salesman he wanted to produce a toy pistol modelled on the Zig Zauer, which had become world-famous; children were clamouring for such a toy. The explanation sounded plausible, and Mr Olaf was the kind who inspired confidence. He presented, as required, a valid Norwegian passport, and the salesman recorded the details. Olaf paid the full price for the weapon, to the delight of the salesman, who in spite of everything did his duty as a Swiss patriot and notified the police. Heinrich immediately realised (with emphasis on the words "immediately" and "realised") that this man was the piece missing from the jigsaw, he drafted in detectives, all the trained manpower he could muster, and set out in pursuit. Mr Olaf arrived at the hotel and ate a lavish Swiss breakfast, doing everything very calmly – and in the Scandinavian way he ate a lot of meat. This isn't in fact such common Scandinavian practice these days. The Vikings on the other hand always ate meat and nothing else – Heinrich displayed his extensive knowledge of history.

Heinrich glanced sidelong at me, to check that I was following the interesting story. He wanted so much to share it with someone and in me he had found the ideal audience, the man naturally more interested in this than in all the other stories in the world, the one most deeply involved in it, the one who enraged him with his frivolous attitude, who was risking his own life and the life of his beloved wife, for no logical reason at all. His scrutiny satisfied him.

Mr Olaf sat at the table overlooking the hotel entrance, saw me and my wife going out, and followed us, leaving a fifty franc note on the table, with the heavy Zig Zauer stuck in his belt, in such a way as not to draw suspicion, while making the weapon easy to draw. Heinrich, who was on the scene and personally shadowing Olaf, signalled to his men and the whole gang set out for the woods in our tracks.

Here I saw fit to interject: "And we, my wife and I, didn't notice anything."

"Appalling carelessness!" he asserted and irrelevantly he added: "You're to leave Switzerland within three days, otherwise, we shall expel you!" – a threat serving as an outlet for his seething anger.

Here my wife came forward, having followed close behind us, not missing a word of Heinrich's story, and announced:

"We're leaving tomorrow."

"The words I longed to hear!" Heinrich exclaimed with relief and hurriedly returned to discharging his burden:

"We covered a lot of ground. When you were close to the clearing, Mr Olsen drew the Zig Zauer, stopped and took aim. You could tell he wasn't born to it, or even properly trained" – he gave a professional opinion and returned to his story:

"I had to think about it for a moment, a long moment. Shooting a man – well, it's easy enough in the movies."

I couldn't agree with him more.

"However," Heinrich continued, "there are situations where there's no other option but to shoot, before the damage is done." It was clear this was the argument which Heinrich meant to raise in reporting to his superiors.

"I drew and I fired," he exclaimed with a light sigh, and added at once, by way of justification: "I'm good at that. Trained. And the thing proved itself. That bastard, Mr Olaf Olsen, fired a hopeless shot, even an amateur could have done better than him, and I scored a bull's-eye from twice the range he shot at you from, and he went down like a shot bird, that's the part that interests you and you're entitled to know it. I'd suggest you don't publicise this or broadcast it. The important thing is that the two of you have survived. I say the two of you," he added, jabbing an accusing finger at me, "because with your irresponsibility you have put your delightful wife in danger too, some intellectual you are!" I expressed my full agreement with a prolonged hmmm...

In the meantime, vehicles were moving into the wood, police vehicles, off-roaders. We returned to our hotel.

My wife burst into tears, I embraced her in a fatherly sort of way and she soon regained her composure. Then she went to the phone and began talking to nameless people in fluent English. I went into the bathroom, feeling the need for a shower, although it was my waistcoat and trousers that were soiled. Leaving the bathroom, I felt much refreshed and began urging my wife to follow my example and freshen up in the shower.

"There's no time for that," she objected.

"Why do you say that?"

"We're going home tomorrow!" she announced.

"What do you mean, we're going home?" I asked with affected innocence and added: "We've got the flight to sort out and all that."

"It's all arranged," she assured me. "Now, you're to phone Shmulik," she demanded.

Without further discussion I picked up the receiver, with Shmulik's visiting-card in front of me.

Somewhere or other, his wife woke him up.

He sounded tense. "We're coming home tomorrow!" I told him and saw fit to add that there had been another attempt on my life. For a moment he was silent and then he responded:

"Maybe it's time after all to sort out that nasty friend of yours!"

"That wouldn't solve anything," I declared with some heat, although I knew I was in the right – "If I were to meet him, that could be infinitely more profitable!" I concluded.

"See you tomorrow!" cried Shmulik, and he hung up.

On the plane there was a party. Champagne was distributed, and a rabbi sitting two rows in front of us, on his way to Israel to spend the holidays there, raised his glass, said a prayer and pronounced a blessing: "Blessed be He who has given us life and has brought us to this time!" I was astonished. I asked my wife: "What is all this? Who ordered the champagne?"

The reply was unequivocal and succinct: "You did!"

We embraced. My wife whispered in my ear: "I sent some to Heinrich and his team too."

In a way that cannot be explained, that was uninvited, my lungs began breathing in a rhythm different from that in which they had breathed hitherto. It began with the row of houses blazing white below me, strewn across arid, overheated land – "We're coming home!" –

I stretched out in my seat. A gate invisible to the eye opened and substitution began, between what was outside it and what was inside. As if the whole of the Bible had put on intangible skin and sinew and passed through this gate. Abraham and Isaac and Jacob and his twelve sons, David and Solomon, Isaiah, Jeremiah, Amos and Elijah. They sprang up in our hearts like something that will never be revealed to the senses and yet exists – was, is, and shall be

It isn't a question of a piece of land but of the spirit, homeland of the spirit, which nothing can impair and which impairs nothing. I was the most fortunate of men and not immune from sorrow, I knew that finally I had found myself in the dazzling light, streaming below me, above me and in me, I knew there were no words capable of expressing this, and yet, I am writing these lines, to spread happiness over the whole world, consummate happiness, which cannot be shared and yet can be lived in such a way that one is an inseparable part of it, happiness which erases all sorrow and above all – cleanses the soul of the last vestige of doubt. All the world has a share in this light of joy, which will not be taken from it, not ever. I was ready, at that moment, to break into song. My wife leaned over and sang *King's Bride* in my ear, understanding my thoughts and bringing them to a conclusion.

The plane began its descent, resembling a

gigantic messenger, bringing with him a thousand tidings of truth for which the world is thirsty, and it shall accept them and be changed.

CHAPTER EIGHTEEN

We returned full of impressions of all kinds and tendencies; this was unlike any other holiday we had ever spent, in that place, and between approximately the same dates, over the past dozen years. Neither of us could say for certain whether this made things better or worse. My wife was firmly of the opinion that events had been bizarre, intervention had been crude and always negative, and henceforward she would be taking more seriously, and certainly paying more attention to – the stories I told her about my past and in particular the warnings I gave, which to her mind had all too often smacked of outright paranoia. I accepted everything submissively, in the solid hope that there might still be unexpected developments in the right direction. On our arrival at Ben-Gurion Airport, another surprise awaited us. After we had collected our baggage we were accosted by a group of ruffians who escorted us to a special department set aside for the reception of V.I.P.s. In the spacious, rather dingy room, we were met by Shmulik, in person. He extended his broad hand and to our utter amazement he apologised, the kind of apology that wasn't at all his normal style. And he didn't just mumble a few barely intelligible words either, as might have been expected, but spoke out with uncharacteristic clarity:

"I'm very sorry, but I had no other way of welcoming you home and wishing you a long life of health and happiness." The words were sincere, with no remaining vestige of the sergeant-major about them.

There's nothing to be said, I thought to myself, the Mossad is pretty efficient when it comes to training its operatives. By way of reply, I spoke a few words of thanks and appreciation, and couldn't resist the temptation to say:

"The Mossad ploughs a deep furrow in its people. If we hadn't met recently, I wouldn't have recognised you!"

"You have to understand, Madam," he said, turning to my wife and ignoring my comment, "we shall need to bother your husband for a few more days, as few as possible, and the bother shouldn't be too troublesome, although as I'm sure you know, the situation is serious, things are hotting up and they must not be allowed under any circumstances" – he stressed the *under any circumstances* and the thought that flashed into my mind was that Shmulik would never make it as a diplomat; the sergeant-major syndrome had left a deep imprint in his soul after all, and deviousness did not come to him naturally; the end of the sentence, addressed to my wife was – "to get out of hand." Our troubles must not under any circumstances be allowed to get out of hand.

This statement on Shmulik's part sounded like a vow, and I had not the shadow of a doubt this was one of the vows that would be kept, in all respects and senses, in the letter and in the spirit.

"And now, I apologise again for the delay I have caused. Go out and meet your reception committee. There seem to be a fair number of people waiting for you. I know – I did some checking-up," he admitted and steered us towards a side-exit – straight into the familiar Israeli maelstrom, the crowd waiting impatiently for returnees from abroad.

It took us a whole week to get ourselves sorted out at home: we put things back in their places, filled the freezer, told friends and relations we were back. At the end of that week, Shmulik phoned.

"I won't ask how you got my phone number" – I was rattled, feeling that my privacy had been violated. "It's supposed to be protected," I added. "All the same, maybe I should learn to be more careful."

"If someone wants to learn, he'll learn," Shmulik retorted, ignoring my bruised sensibilities. "The secret of learning is to leave behind any kind of conceit, and take on a little humility – however little it may be."

"I agree with every word of that," I conceded sincerely. "But I still want to know who leaked you my number," I demanded, without any real hope.

"The phone company," was the answer.

"How?" I asked, although I realised my question was superfluous.

"There's a certain hierarchy in every properly run state," Shmulik explained patiently. "One official service defers to another official service, and this deference is sanctioned by higher authority in the public interest."

"I'm well aware of all that," I assured him. Shmulik changed the subject and arranged a meeting at a time convenient to me, which he reckoned was eleven in the morning, in a café on Ben Yehuda Street, Tel Aviv.

We met, had something to drink, and a snack of some kind. He paid, and made a point of getting a receipt. I asked if it was at his employer's expense. He nodded. Our conversation was both practical and succinct. Shmulik began by asking me again if the elimination of Amin Abu Halil would lead, in my opinion, to the eradication of the plague. My unequivocal answer, after thorough consideration lasting some five minutes, was "No!"

"For the time being you've saved his life," Shmulik commented with a faint smile and added: "I'll make sure he gets to hear of it."

I couldn't restrain my curiosity, and I asked Shmulik again about the man who saved *my* life.

Shmulik smiled a broad, unexpected and magnanimous smile, transforming the expression on his face beyond recognition – from dour austerity to a look of fatherly understanding, and willingness to oblige. "Your gratitude has been passed on," he began, "and if you want to know more of his particulars...

"He's a Polish Jew in his early thirties, who did his army service in Poland. He did not get on with his sergeant-major, a tough guy who hated Jews – it was like an intoxicating drug in his blood-stream. He knew all the derogatory terms for Jews in all languages and dialects and enjoyed applying them to Mr Atlas. Mr Atlas's first name was Saul, or according to the translation of the Christian scriptures – Paul. This was the name he adopted. On manoeuvres with the Polish army, he put a bullet in the sergeant-major's thick skull with a revolver fired from long range, and then deserted. He turned up in Paris and became a professional hitman, hanging out with underground types at the "Poule" – that's what they call the basement café in the centre of Paris. Naturally, he has a sentimental attachment to his persecuted race, and he's the one we usually turn to. Your story impressed him. Incidentally, he sends you this greeting: 'Enjoy life and don't sell yourself short'." Suddenly he returned to the subject that interested him most: "Never mind that, what in your opinion is likely to halt this disease – meaning, besides identifying it. The medical establishment is baffled by the diagnosis that's been thrown at it so readily, and has no rational explanation for it, or any hope of a rational explanation. Doctors are strangely reluctant to go anywhere near Hasda, and the same applies to all the ancillary services too, so if you can think of any way of halting the spread of the disease, or alleviating the symptoms, anything at all, let's hear it. We can't afford to lose the battle with the crude racism that's in the ascendant now, getting stronger all the time and threatening to take us all over, whatever the outcome is going to be. We have no mercy to look forward to, and it seems the only one we can trust – is God."

"I suppose you have read some other books, besides *Erral*," was my comment.

"The point has been made, that homework is needed, and anyone as thoroughgoing as me does this in depth, not missing any crevice, as everyone has to do everything he possibly can, to stop this volcano that's erupting and going on erupting..." He fell silent. I took the hint.

"I very much hope you're not pushed for time," he added – it was part question, part statement.

"I've done everything I can to free up as much time as possible."

"You've done the right thing," Shmulik concluded, and after a couple of minutes of concentrated thought he asked: "Tell me everything you know about Rocky Mountain spotted fever, in as much depth as possible and from all angles. Sometimes the insight of the layman can uncover things that the experts and self-styled pundits are incapable of grasping, simply because they are experts and self-styled pundits. I assume you're familiar with the disease and its causes."

"Very much so," I told him truthfully, and went on to explain: "Well then, the disease is caused by a micro-organism that isn't a bacterium and isn't a virus, and is called 'Rickettsia" after the man who discovered it – Howard Taylor Ricketts."

His notebook in his left hand, and his right scribbling away at furious speed, Shmulik asked for clarification: "What is the difference between a bacterium and a virus, and what are the distinguishing features of Rickettsia?"

"A virus can pass through bacterial filters, something totally impossible for a bacterium. A virus proliferates on a medium of living cells, while a bacterium readily proliferates on a normal medium."

"And where does Rickettsia fit in here?"

"It doesn't pass through bacterial filters."

"And in that respect it resembles a bacterium" Shmulik deduced. I nodded.

"It proliferates on living cells."

"And thus it resembles a virus" Shmulik concluded.

To save time, I made no reference to his highly commendable perspicacity. I went on to say: "Antibiotics destroy bacteria, but they have no effect on viruses. For Rickettsia, no effective antibiotic agent has yet been discovered. There have been suggestions that chloromphenicol might be of some use. All these facts are known to us thanks to the hard work put in by Ricketts, who transmitted the disease from infected to healthy animals, and isolated Rickettsia not only of the sick animals but also of ticks and their eggs. And thus he has proved this is a natural channel of transmission. A tick infected with Rickettsia attaches itself to a host, and infects it with R.M.S.F. The cycle of infection, on the basis of the bite of a tick carrying Rickettsia, includes human beings, with all the implications resulting from that. Ricketts made another step forward, when he proved that very few humans infected by R.M.S.F., only ten percent of them, have any immunity to it. But he was unable, in live experiments, to create antibodies. Ninety per cent of sufferers from R.M.S.F. die. To this day, as far as I know, there has been no success in using animals to create antibodies to Rickettsia rickettsii, which causes R.M.S.F.

"Cultures of Rickettsia can be grown in human blood, until they become dependent on this particular blood – in other words, they only attack this type of blood. Just now, Doctor Amin has made them dependent on a certain type of human blood, bearing certain D.N.A., the D.N.A. of Jews. Those Rickettsias won't proliferate in any other blood, and therefore they will attack and damage only those whose blood is Jewish."

"Isn't it possible to make them dependent on other blood – Arab blood for example?" Shmulik asked.

"It certainly is possible, if Arab or other blood carries D.N.A. different from that of any other blood. In fact it would be quite feasible, it seems to me, to make it dependent on all types of human blood."

"And then the whole of humanity will be wiped out," Shmulik hissed.

"Wiped out is a bit of an overstatement," I commented.

"Thanks very much for the concise lecture. It seems to me," Shmulik continued, "that by investing effort worthy of the name it should be possible to come up with something that will halt this infernal disease. By the way, the offer of a post in the Nes Ziona laboratories is still open..."

"Thankyou very much," I thanked him wholeheartedly, but I'm not interested."

"Don't forget, you could be drafted!"

"That never does anyone any good," I replied, rejecting the threat, "but I think there are things that can be done."

"We shall do and listen," Shmulik declared, quoting the Bible.

"I'm going to meet Amin Abu Halil," I said, taking up the cue that he wanted me to take up.

"That shall be done!" Shmulik declared, with a return to his sergeant-major's manner, and after a moment of silence he added:

"Your good friend is currently living in Berlin. As I told you before, he's married to Hilde, granddaughter of a Nazi general, who died alongside Adolf Hitler. The energetic Amin has already made his lady pregnant. They're expecting a baby. You're to go to Berlin. You know the address. The happy couple are living in the general's house. Frau Hilde has a sister called Erika, who lives in a separate apartment in the same building, the late general's property. Fraulein Erika is a spinster, and apparently man-hungry. You can start breaking down the walls with her. Come back here tomorrow, we'll drink some more of this vile coffee and eat some more stale buns, and you'll get all the information you need."

I nodded in assent. I sensed his satisfaction, which he made no attempt to conceal.

"If all goes according to plan," he went on to say, "the day after tomorrow, you'll be walking the streets of Berlin. Don't take any excess baggage, you don't need it."

Shmulik stood up, held out his hand in valediction. "Tomorrow," he said, "same time, same place."

My wife was not best pleased on hearing the news, but she realised that no argument, however acute and persuasive it might be, could compete with the accumulation of facts.

"Watch out for those German women!" she made a point of warning me.

"By the grace of God we shall do our best."

"Amen to that!" was her blessing.

CHAPTER NINETEEN

From Shmulik I received a ticket for a Lufthansa flight, business class: a window seat, comfort guaranteed. Next day, carrying just a light suitcase, I was driven to the airport. My wife came to see me off and after a brief conversation we parted. The flight was smooth, and could be described as pleasant and agreeable. It seemed the stewardesses had agreed (or been asked?) to take special care of me, with the kind of womanly concern universally reserved for an attractive man (I knew I hardly qualified as that).

In Berlin I boarded a taxi, and gave the address, which I had memorised. The driver dropped me off, at midday, beside a tall and somewhat antiquated building, reminiscent of a watchtower on a medieval city wall. A listed red-brick building, protected by a pair of cumbersome doors, constructed from heavy Teutonic timber, extravagantly carved. I stood on the opposite side from the house on Humboldt Strasse, Number 19. No doubt, I looked strange to the passers-by, as well as to the residents of the old house, rising to a height which with some slight exaggeration could be described as great, and containing no more than three modern storeys. I didn't want to waste any time. On the contrary, all I wanted was to get the job done in the minimum time possible, not a particularly encouraging omen for the success of the mission, but I decided to take the risk and I really didn't care that much. The tenants of the house in question didn't seem to be on edge in anticipation of some attack coming from outside, on the part of a (hitherto) unseen enemy.

I leaned my case against the decidedly modern wall of the house facing Number 19 Humboldt Strasse, and there was nothing old about this one: fenced like the house opposite with a low wall, but freshly whitewashed, and gleaming white. The sun beat down with the harsh light of late summer on the old house, and I was lucky to be standing in the shade and not exposed to the full force of the rays, which would have been quite capable of microwaving matza bread. I waited. An hour passed, and still no one showed any interest in me. From the whitewashed house behind me, a portly, dignified German gentleman emerged, in a blue suit, blue shirt with white stripes, and a big blue bow-tie, matching his eyes. He looked like a business partner in some corporate institution, hurrying to his work-place, not far away, with heavy tread – indicative of age and lack of interest in his work. No doubt looking forward impatiently to his date of retirement and planning a round-the-world cruise in the company of his wife or alone. About twenty minutes after him, a woman built on generous lines came out, evidently his wife, and turned in the opposite direction to that taken by the man, behaviour perhaps symbolic of the total lack of understanding between the embittered pair, who have stopped asking questions and stopped arguing – while each cherishes secret expectations of the departure of the other. And then one of the heavy doors opposite opened, and a large-limbed woman, heavily pregnant (Hilde, I guessed), came out, waited for about ten minutes, stopped a taxi and disappeared inside it. The taxi sped away, in whatever direction she had asked for.

I felt as if my heart was beating with redoubled force, and it seemed to be trying to climb up my throat and moisten my mouth which had dried. The heavy door swung open again, closely followed by the matching door. A new Audi, skilfully driven by a young woman (Erika, was the logical supposition) left the house, in no particular haste. I began following it on foot, an act of desperation, and then the taxi I was hoping for hooted behind me. I stopped, got in and asked the driver to follow the receding Audi. He did so, looking less than absolutely enthusiastic. The Audi stopped in a huge parking lot outside a pub, brightly lit in the middle of the day, a gesture of cheap extravagance. I asked the driver to pull up, got down and paid. The tip brought a smile to his face, scored with deep wrinkles, which did not betray his age.

The driver wished me "Good hunting!"

I went into the pub and soon located the "subject", or what in Bulgaria we used to call the "object". This was a pleasantly shaped young woman, somewhat reminiscent of the lady who left the house before her, the pregnant one. This resemblance encouraged me. I sat down some distance from her and watched every move she made. She ordered calvados, a French drink distilled from the juice of apples, not powerful enough to cast you into the void of oblivion or even to induce mild intoxication.

So, she had no intention of getting drunk. This was my first assumption, and I knew it wasn't to be trusted. I ordered myself a small calvados, doing everything possible to avoid drawing attention, on the part of those seated at the bar, the few sitting at tables, those entering and leaving or the barman, who in obedience to his rules of professional etiquette, immediately expressed curiosity and asked where I was from and all the rest of it. The German that I learned in high school and improved more or less on holidays in Switzerland proved its worth and I succeeded in cooling his curiosity, sending a message that I wasn't interested in any conversation. The barman was experienced, he understood, served the calvados without further ado and moved away from me.

The "object" ordered beer – meaning, she was thirsty, as simple as that. This was followed by a small brandy. The calvados had just been the camouflaged opening gambit. Camouflaged from whom? I reassured myself and decided with uncharacteristic optimism, from herself. It was a long time since I last drank beer and I didn't want to drink it now, but the barman was approaching and if I wanted not to attract attention, I had to order something.

"Beer!" I saw the barman's curiosity soaring to new heights. His brown eyes clouded over. He put the glass down in front of me with a slam that said a great deal. As far as I was concerned the meaning was: Stop pissing about! If you're going to do something, get on with it! I answered myself: Yes, I am going to do something, really! And I meant it, grasping my almost desperate situation, my time that was running out, and my determination to complete the assignment in the best way possible and as quickly as possible and go home satisfied. On assessing the situation, it seemed all these objectives were remote and yet, as somebody told me, things that are remote are not necessarily unattainable, and there was no doubt that when the moment came, I would dive in at the deep end, whatever the outcome. On the other hand, I consoled myself – don't exaggerate, what outcome are you talking about? Here there's a woman who's bored if not more than that and any man who dares will get everything he wants from her. Including information. All the information she's capable of supplying. The lady ordered tequila and this struck me as dangerous; it seemed she was after all intent on getting drunk and "forgetting it all", rendering herself incapable of distinguishing between reality and unreality, and entangling herself and me in stories, just as likely to be fiction as fact.

Without giving much thought to what I was doing, I picked up the half-empty glass with the contents that only made me feel nauseous, sat down beside her and muttered a few words of apology, which I meant sincerely, for staring at her these last few minutes, an attractive young woman, trying to forget something – as indeed I was. I just had this fantastic idea that maybe I could help her somehow, and with a little goodwill, maybe she could help me too.

The response came more quickly than I expected, and all of it was a surprise.

"Sir, there's no need to sniff around me...

it's true that I'm young and attractive and in bed I'm a thousand times younger and a thousand times more attractive, and you think a good fuck will do both of us good... maybe you're right, maybe not... I've had my share of bitter disappointments. Come on, let's take a closer look at you." She moved her bar-stool slightly and our eyes met. Her eyes were like the eyes of a hungry leopard, or leopardess I should say, on heat and ready to explode. I didn't know how I looked to her, but she didn't hesitate to tell me – "You look small to me, too small to jump into bed with me, although quite often the little ones can be a surprise... You aren't local, Asiatic I'd say," she added, showing astonishing intuition. "I'm guessing, though I rather wish I wasn't," she went on effusively, "that you're from Israel and you haven't come here just to chat me up and offer me a fuck, you want to milk me for information..."

"My brother-in-law is an Arab, and he's done something very nasty to you people, and being the kind of guy he is, he's very proud of it. And you want to know all about it. Listen carefully, little Israeli that you are. I'm the granddaughter of a Nazi general. What this means is, I'm as full as a pomegranate with guilt-feelings of all shapes and colours, and I'm prepared to do anything to atone a little, to ease the burden on me and on my conscience. Come on, let's go to my apartment." She left a note on the counter and slid off her stool with its round seat upholstered in black leather, and I did likewise and followed her out of the pub, like a horny tomcat that's had a bucket of icy water thrown over it. I joined her in the Audi, and no more than five minutes later we arrived at Number 19 Humboldt Strasse. I got out to help her, opening and closing the gates, and all this without a word exchanged between us. She led the way, running up the creaking wooden spiral staircase, like the staircases of watchtowers since time immemorial. Admittedly, her apartment wasn't built like a fortress, but was like any other apartment anywhere in the world – modestly proportioned, with three medium-sized rooms.

When we reached the apartment, still panting after the climb up three storeys and three flights of spiral staircase, she apologised profusely for the lack of a lift, but added that she preferred things the way they were, the air of down-at-heel antiquity and the memories that the thick wall had absorbed. She offered me a glass of brandy, took one for herself and without any ceremony, emptied the glass at one gulp and put it down on the old, round, mahogany table, laden with heavy boxes in polished walnut wood, and sensing my embarrassment she surprised me with a toast in pure Ashkenazi: "Lehaim!" and invited me to taste the amber liquid. Seeing no other way out of my awkward predicament, I did as she suggested.

"You may be surprised to hear that my surname, like the name of the street I'm living in, isn't accidental," she assured me. "You must have learnt in your geography lessons at school about the brothers Alexander and Wilhelm Humboldt, who made a very significant contribution to the science of geography – what do they call it? – physical geography and bio-geography – and about their 'murderous' grandmother who brought them up, who used to drag them out of bed on frozen winter nights and force them to wrestle half-naked in the yard at the back of our house, and that way she toughened them up for their adventures around the world in the service of science. The two brothers explored the North Pole."

"It wasn't the North Pole, or the South," I corrected her – "but the lower Amazon and the estuary of the Orinoco"

"As you see," she responded, "my soul is the soul of an artist. Humble details mean nothing to me. Besides my German body, and my sexual proclivities – I don't even have half of a German gene!" she stressed proudly, in a tone brooking no disagreement. "And there was a Frenchman with them too," she added off-handedly, "I've forgotten his name."

"Bonpland," I reminded her.

"What a memory you have!" – she was genuinely impressed. "With the limited technical means available to them at that time," she continued, reverting to the main topic, "they achieved so much and returned to their homeland garlanded with worldwide renown, just as their grandmother wanted. At the beginning of the twentieth century, the municipality of Berlin decided to call the street where the Humboldt brothers lived by their name.

"The brothers were in love, both of them, with their charming and succulent neighbour, Erika," she went on to say. "Despite the meticulous, vulpine you could almost call it, supervision on the part of their grandmother, they nearly fought a duel over her. Erika was pregnant by one of them, to this day no one knows which, and she gave birth to my grandfather, who had the same kind of Spartan upbringing, according to the rules laid down by his great grandmother. He was drafted into the army, and he was a colonel during the First World War. Hitler impressed him and he soon became one of his most loyal generals, utterly loyal and a talented tactician as well, the bitter rival of Guderian, the tank supremo. Anyway, he was one of Hitler's closest adherents and most committed acolytes. He killed himself the moment he heard the Fuhrer had done the same in his bunker.

"As his granddaughter, I fervently hope he has found some peace, at least in the other world. My grandfather was a man with a conscience and he suffered torments over everything that he was obliged to do in the Second World War, on the orders of the Fuhrer whom he admired, but he went ahead and did it anyway, and he knew what others were doing and was a witness to their actions. A thoroughly tragic figure. Again, I express the hope that his tragic, tormented soul finds eternal rest!"

"Amen to that!" I chimed in – on an obsequious impulse, lacking full conviction.

"I thank you for that endorsement," she responded. She executed a dancer's twirl in the narrow space of the room, and to my surprise stopped in front of me and proceeded to say: "Obviously you want to fuck me – and I'm no less keen on the idea. As I'm sure you know, the Nordic race is drawn by a fatal attraction towards the inferior races, the Asiatics, the degenerate Semitic race of the Middle East. You can do this in whatever way appeals to you." And so saying, she began to strip.

She had an athletic, well-developed body: solid thighs, a typically Teutonic arse, that managed to be broad and pert at the same time – utterly irresistible (the way a Panzer tank is irresistible), and a bust that scythed the air with every movement.

"Come on, let's not pretend," she cajoled me in a perky tone. "What I really like is when people call me filthy names and shout obscenities at me. I'm sure you know those kinds of words, in any language you like. Amin used to call me a name, in Arabic, that he refused to translate – *sharmuta* – and he combined it with German words, saying I was *Die grosste schmutzigste Sharmuta in der ganze Welt*. You'd be doing me a real favour if you could enlighten me. Do you know any Arabic?"

"The basics," I replied.

"And this word?"

"Yes, my knowledge extends that far."

"So what does it mean?"

"Whore. So the whole of that phrase means, The biggest and filthiest whore in all the world," I explained.

She moved closer to me and started undressing me the way you undress a baby.

"What I don't get," she commented, "is why you're being so resistant. I'm not a cannibal or anything like that, so why are you opposed to this? Don't you fancy me? And if Amin's right and I'm a whore, you can have the best sex ever, as the English call it – and all free of charge. You still haven't answered my question, why you're resisting. You're not a virgin, I can tell the difference between virgins and non-virgins, and it doesn't look like you've got syphilis, clap or Aids..."

"I'm married," I retorted.

"And you're afraid of your wife?" she

laughed.

"I respect her," I amended.

"After you've been with me, you'll respect her all the more, and she'll respect me too. The way my sister Hilde has respected me, ever since I did it with her husband. Incidentally, it made him feel great and he cursed me with all the English curses he knows, and there's plenty of them, plus some German ones he'd picked up, and Arabic of course. And that's a sure sign that he got full satisfaction, better than anything he's known in the past or is likely to know in the future. And now, you can curse me in your language, in classical Hebrew, the language of the Scriptures."

"There aren't many curses there," I replied.

"What a dismal language!" she declared categorically. "Go on, make a start!" she demanded, the kind of demand that's not easily evaded.

"Stinking bitch!" – I offered, and was immediately asked to translate it. The translation merited some textual analysis:

"Bitch yes, stinking – no! Surely you know the Germans are the cleanest race on earth. Three showers a day with special soaps, as you'll see soon enough... I love the pungent smell of a real man. It sets my whole being in a spin, floods me with hormones, an unstoppable flow. Got any more?"

"Stupid bloody Nazi!"

"That's a good one," she declared, "you're getting the idea."

Underwear fell. I was led with unreasonable force to the bed. "Let's go!" she urged me. I found myself spread-eagled on the double bed with her gigantic body entwining around mine in every conceivable and inconceivable posture, all positions without exception, some of them surprising and some of them ominous.

"I haven't had enough of your curses yet."

"Arse-licker!" I gasped.

"Outstanding!" she moaned.

After the first round, came the second. And then – the warriors' rest, or I should say, the woman-warrior's rest.

"You're better than him!" – she pointed downstairs with her thumb.

"You're not!" I retorted.

"Who am I not better than?"

"My wife!"

"You look like someone who's stepped out of a long and mind-numbingly boring romantic poem from the eighteenth century! At least you've made me experience something I wouldn't have believed existed."

"You and me both," I responded illogically.

"I'm glad to hear it! And what have you experienced?" she demanded to know, in typical style.

"The Teutonic Kriemhilde or Brunnhilde,

not the Wagnerian ones – but the real thing."

"And I've experienced King Solomon, not the Biblical one, but the real thing," she responded appropriately, and added: "The time has come to replenish our unromantic systems with the million calories we have burnt up!"

And so we did. We showered, dressed, ate sandwiches, drank vermouth and stood steadily on our feet. It was then that she surprised me with a sudden outburst:

"You," she jabbed a menacing finger at me, "are nothing other than the rusty relic of total misunderstanding of the times we are living in!"

"Could you elucidate that?" I demanded.

"Open your ears wide and listen. Our age is the inverted age. The age that came before was the age of the way to eternal life and the blueprint was simple and clear: don't lie, don't fornicate, don't pursue gain, don't complain. And it didn't work – because human beings are designed to lie, to fornicate, to pursue gain and pity themselves, and it doesn't matter what anyone says. In the inverted age, man lies, fornicates, pursues gain and finds legitimate satisfaction in self-pity, and has two claims to make: one, he can't abide by the above-mentioned rules, and the other, he doesn't believe in eternal life and doesn't want it anyway. He is addicted and dependent, utterly and willingly dependent, on his anatomical body, and he's not prepared under any circumstances to forgo its transient delights."

"The former age is over and gone and it left a lot of scars. Mankind is fed up with scars. Our age lives the moment, the only thing that it's left with after the bitter disappointments it has absorbed. People are killed suddenly, innocent people. You and your compatriots should know this better than most. Come on, let's live the fleeting moment, and leave eternity to the self-righteous. In our age we know how to squeeze out the last atom of sensual pleasure. The inverted age is the cannibal age, and humanity enjoys being cannibal, it wants to be cannibal. It's capable of this and knows it. It has shaken off the dumb Freudianism of Jewish guilt."

"What guilt are you talking about, and for what?" I interjected.

"For the Crucifixion!"

I had no answer to this.

"To make your job easier you can do whatever you like with me, even kill me and rip out my guts or sacrifice them to the idols. I'm making you an offer of incomparable generosity and magnitude: be a cannibal, true saint of our age, the inverted age that is."

"You're saying the weirdest things and they are nothing more than the snapshot of a situation, without any hope, without inspiration, without truth."

"I heard of a Turk, who claimed that the world is wallowing in blood because of women who aren't getting sexual satisfaction, and this loads the air with hostility and poison and bitterness – a convenient, logical and reliable springboard for disputes, quarrels, wars and cruelty for its own sake... there's more than a grain of truth in this... so please do me a favour, kind Sir," – turning to me – "and give satisfaction to this volcano of hormones, and you'll be making your modest contribution to the salvation of the world! You are most cordially invited," she saw fit to stress.

"Thankyou. I have some questions to ask you."

"Ask, and I shall answer to the best of my ability and beyond."

"How can you answer beyond your ability?" I asked, not inclined to allow any evasion.

"If you discover what's hidden behind the question and go further and deeper. I'm sure all your questions have to do with Amin."

"So that's an example of going further and deeper!" I declared.

"Go on then, ask."

"What does he talk about? Has he been agitated lately?"

"He's more agitated than any other time since I've known him. And all his conversations revolve around one single axis – the destruction of the Jews. My learned brother-in-law asserts that God has put into his hands the clean, sophisticated and purely scientific means of bringing about the end, once and for all, of Jews and of Judaism, without any harm resulting from this to anyone who isn't Jewish. When he said this I couldn't resist suggesting, in all seriousness, he should go and consult a shrink, immediately if not sooner, preferably a shrink with a sound reputation, and I was prepared to pay the costs of consultation and psychiatric treatment, the best that's available in Germany."

"And how did he react?" I interjected, wanting to save time and bring her back to the main issue.

"You could have no idea! Do you want three guesses?"

"OK, but not just now. I'm agog with curiosity, more so than anything I've known since I was ten years old, and I want to hear the facts. So, how did he react to your frank comments?"

"With three simple words," Erika conceded.

"And those words were?" I prompted her.

"You are right!"

I wasn't satisfied with this. I waited and Erika didn't disappoint.

"A few days ago," she continued, controlling her impulses, "Amin went on to say: Now I have to plan, in all seriousness, bearing in mind the presence of that accursed race in all corners of the world, to ensure that my bacterium gets there, and does its job.

You'll need millions to do that, I told him. That's where you're wrong, he said, Not millions – billions, and I've got them!

"That's all I can tell you up to now... if there's any more to come, you'll hear it from me. An insignificant payment for the fuck that you were so opposed to. You know my address and you've got my phone number. I don't know anything about you... maybe it's better that way. You can come looking for me. Once a week at least." She smiled a broad, bright, surprising smile.

"Thankyou very much, Erika!" I thanked her wholeheartedly.

CHAPTER TWENTY

I left the apartment. I returned later that evening, and asked a favour, with all the courtesy which the English language affords:

"Erika, I'd like to meet Amin."

"Is it urgent?" she asked, with all the solemn dignity she was capable of.

"Urgent!" I confirmed in a tone which almost scaled the heights of German brusqueness.

"I'll go down at once and find out for you. Is it OK to tell him you're here?"

"It's OK."

She returned about an hour later, agitated to the roots of her flaxen hair.

"He came close to bursting into tears! He says he's dying to meet you as soon as possible. Something else he mentioned, like an afterthought – he reckons he owes you his life. It seems there's a grain of truth in it."

"More than a grain of truth!" I thought it

appropriate to stress, remembering Shmulik's words: "I'll make sure he gets to hear of it." Half an hour later I was invited into the downstairs flat. A spacious flat. I was ushered into the sitting-room. There were a number of broad, deep-seated armchairs, some with foot-stools, upholstered in provocative and repellent purple velvet, like blood and perhaps fire too. A long and heavy table, highly polished, a grand piano in the eastern corner. A jumble of photographs and pictures, mounted on dark green card. A grandiose salon indeed! There were paintings too: some classical prints and also examples of work by the leading artists of the Twentieth Century – the century we were all glad to see the back of. The pregnant Hilde, very like her unruly sister, and just as capable of being unruly herself, were she not inhibited by her swollen belly – sat in the western corner, furthest from the piano. I was invited to sit in one of the armchairs, which to my surprise proved to be very comfortable. Amin appeared out of nowhere, clicked his heels, German officer style, held out a familiar, bony hand, which I shook with genuine warmth, and sat down facing me in a matching chair. I scrutinised him, with curiosity. He had hardly changed. His face had grown thin and his big sad eyes protruded. We both sank into the soft upholstery, fit to dispel any troublesome thought. Hilde disappeared somewhere, evidently to a concealed kitchen, reappearing a few moments later pulling a tea-trolley, its two shelves laden to overflowing with cakes, sandwiches, thinly-sliced bread, saucers of butter and various kinds of jam. The drinks on offer were mineral water, coffee and tea. Amin apologised for not serving alcohol, in accordance with his religious obligations, but said he could offer me a can of beer or a glass of wine or brandy if I chose, although – and here he smiled a smile devoid of any pretence – to the best of his knowledge, I was not an outstanding aficionado of hard liquor, of any kind or strength.

"Your memory isn't failing you," I confirmed.

"Not yet," he rejoined, as if to take some of the gloss away from my compliment.

I drank a little tea, with its warming and encouraging influence, which I needed so much. I took a dry, unostentatious biscuit. He poured himself coffee, and took some of the same biscuits.

"A proper English high tea!" he declared, feeling the need to say something.

"The English and their customs!" I responded, for the same reason.

"Take their customs away, and they wouldn't be English any more!" he concluded.

"We admire them so much," I continued in the same vein.

"It's better and nicer that way," Amin

chimed in. I sipped more of my tea. I held the cup in both hands, to warm them, as a way of overcoming my embarrassment, an effort which proved eminently successful.

"So," I began, "you've done what you threatened to do!"

"And you have to believe me," he countered with some warmth, "I'm very sorry for this!"

I could not restrain my professional curiosity – even if I had wanted to – and without any diplomatic preambles, I demanded brusquely:

"Who did you get the Rickettsias from?"

It seemed he sensed the turmoil inside me and evidently, despite his regret which apparently sincere, clear and emphatic – he was proud of his achievement.

"From the university lab."

"They don't just give away lethal micro-organisms. That's strictly and absolutely forbidden."

"I still got the stuff."

"How?" I controlled myself in an effort not to risk losing the information, which interested me very much.

"Through Miss Davenport."

"The laboratory superintendent?" – it was more of a statement than a question.

This was an elderly spinster, who managed the laboratories at the University of Columbia, a perfectionist and a pedant who could reduce strong men to tears, acutely conscious of the weight of responsibility laid on her narrow shoulders and the salary she earned. A lady with a distinguished family pedigree, dating back to the legendary Mayflower.

"How did you do that?" I pressed him, although I sensed he was just as eager to share his stunning scientific achievements as I was to hear about them.

"I made love to her."

"But she's over sixty!" I marvelled. "And you know," I couldn't resist adding, "if this ever comes to light she'll be dismissed, in disgrace and without entitlement to any pension."

"It won't come to light," he declared firmly and added, "I'm not going to tell, and neither are you!"

"That's right," I confirmed.

"What is right anyway?" – he poured out his bitterness.

"Right, is what leads the wrongdoer to full repentance."

"And who is the judge of what is right?" he fired another bullet.

"Only God."

"In other words," he persisted – "mankind has neither the right nor the ability to form a just judgment."

"Absolutely so, and in all circumstances!" was the categorical answer.

"And why is that?"

"Because you will find no human being who has not sinned, has not committed some offence, from a white lie to violent murder, in his imagination or in reality, which amount to the same thing."

"How is the justice of God attained?"

"By not interfering with His business and His activities."

"And how is that done?"

"By earning the privilege of believing in Him, adhering to Him, trusting in Him."

"In other words – the one who believes in Him, adheres to Him and trusts in Him, has nothing to fear or to complain about!"

"Exactly," I concurred.

"From which it follows, that every dispute between neighbours, relatives and peoples, even our two peoples, will come to its full and comprehensive resolution, in direct proportion to faith, adherence and trust in God."

"Which are directly opposed to hatred, vengefulness and arrogance."

"So what we have to do, is dispel hatred, vengefulness and arrogance!"

"That is the truth," I responded emphatically.

I returned to the topic that interested me.

"How did you keep the Rickettsia?" – my curiosity was overflowing.

"It went through a process of adaptation."

"You mean, you don't depend any more on Rocky Mountain deer..."

He completed the sentence for me:

"But on the stray dogs of New York City."

"You've been working hard," I declared.

"I had outstanding assistants."

"Half a dozen elderly New York virgins?"

"Perish the thought!" he protested, "A full dozen young Arabs, studying in higher education institutions across the USA. They all studied life sciences or medicine. They answered the call. They left the lecture-hall bench and moved to a house that I rented. We opened what amounted to boarding kennels, and they helped with the work which wasn't free of serious danger, the risk of death. They knew this and worked tirelessly, with commendable enthusiasm. Soon, the dogs started dying of Rocky Mountain fever, suffering terribly. It was a shocking spectacle. We had to ensure that the ticks, causing the sickness and death of the dogs, could be transferred to new dogs."

"How did you do this?"

"We enabled uninfected dogs to come into the closest possible contact with infected or dead dogs. And we were entirely successful."

"Those bastard ticks did the job for you!" I declared.

"That's true, of course. Ticks, as you know, sense the warmth of the victim approaching and attach themselves to it in any way possible. We buried scores of dogs.

"The next stage was the most repellent and dangerous. We had to transfer infected ticks to plastic containers, with air supply, and on to the main testing station, meaning of course, the village of Hasda in Galilee. And here the most decisive phase took place: adaptation of Rickettsia on the basis of Jewish D.N.A."

"You must have needed massive quantities of Jewish blood!" I commented with a certain sense of pride.

"True," Amin concurred – "and where was I going to find it if not in the place with the world's highest concentration of Jews, in Israel."

"Stocks of blood in Israel's hospitals," I offered a superficial guess.

"Bull's-eye!" Amin commended my superficiality, and continued:

"The transfer was smooth. In Israel the dogs were distributed, free, to the Jewish families and also to the Arab families in Hasda."

"In both Judaism and Islam, the dog is considered an unclean creature."

"The rumour was spread, that progress and unity demanded the rearing of dogs and their treatment with the appropriate degree of respect. It was hinted to the Arabs that love of their homeland required this, it was a form of holy war, the Jihad. The Jews, seeing themselves as equals to the Arabs in every respect, could not conceive the possibility of lagging behind the Arabs, with their understanding of dogs. The ticks, doing what comes naturally, also passed on to human beings, the ones tending the dogs, infected them with Rickettsias and the results were publicised in the media... not in an appropriately scientific form of course" – he could not conceal a sense of professional pride.

"How many 'passages' did it take to reach dependence?" I asked.

"Nine to twelve," the answer came.

"Did you use a liquid or solid medium?"

"Exclusively liquid," he replied, "although I would have preferred to work with solids. The way I did it was time consuming, caused a lot of complications and raised all kinds of question-marks. But I had no choice."

"Did you have control checks?" I returned to the subject, barely daring to hope that the experiment had not been properly conducted, such that the results on the ground would be discredited and the whole murderous theory invalidated.

"Arab blood donated free of charge, European blood – at full market price."

"The Europeans didn't ask what was the purpose of the research?"

"All they asked for was payment in dollars and within twenty-four hours."

"You're talking about hospitals in the European capitals?"

"Berlin, Paris, Rome – the best hospitals," he replied briefly, a reply that embarrassed him too, though it hardly amounted to a trauma.

"The results?" I demanded to know and he wasn't slow to inform me:

"Without Jewish blood – the Rickettsias die, disintegrate and disappear."

"Bingo!" I couldn't resist saying, "Fantastic!"

"It's pure micro-biological science."

"An impressive piece of work," I couldn't help but tell the truth.

"I won't be a candidate for the Nobel Peace Prize," he retorted reluctantly, "and you have to believe me, I greatly regret all this and I apologise most sincerely."

I gave him a keen look. His brown, almost swarthy eyes, his face, so Arab in all its sharp lines, made him the epitome of the proud and pure-bred son of the Arab race, warrior and enthusiast, the conqueror who doesn't know how to treat those he has conquered and how to hold on to his conquests, the religious fanatic, bowing devoutly five times a day in the direction of Mecca, praising his God and thanking Him for the very air he breathes. Since I said nothing, Amin took the opportunity to back up his words and clarify them to some extent.

"We never had the suffering of any human being on our conscience, irrespective of race or nationality. In fact, I believed the conscience was a Jewish-western invention, with its roots in flawed personality, misunderstanding of responsibility and absence of faith. And then suddenly something crops up, devil or angel, I still don't know which, and hits me in the chest, right here in the chest, where my heart's supposed to be. A physical blow, and this heart starts missing beats or the opposite, working double time and racing like a runaway horse, without a rider. And I wish I could turn the wheel backwards, but God has imposed on us the ineluctable rule that the wheel cannot be reversed once it is rolling down the slope, so we must learn to be more cautious in the future. I should say, so we must learn to guard against arrogance. Suddenly I began to understand the world of *Subhan Ismo!*" He glanced at me quickly to see if the benediction was familiar to me, and went on to say, "I saw the pictures in the paper. The children who died of the plague. On TV they screened horrific images of the dying and for the first time in my life, this was not a nice experience for me!"

"You mean, the fact that they were Jewish and not Arab children?" I demanded clarification, to gain a deeper understanding of the bitterness infecting his soul.

"Exactly so!" he declared in typically peremptory style that meant – I have changed from the person I have been since birth. "Besides this," he added, "there's no guarantee that tomorrow this will not be inflicted on other children – English, Indian, African, Arab..." his words sounded convincing.

At this point I couldn't resist the impulse to say: "His Name be blessed" - the direct translation of the Arabic *Subhan Ismo*

He pondered this and added the response: "His Name be blessed for ever and to all eternity!"

I felt tears in my throat. I turned to him again:

"I can say to you in all sincerity, that I see in you more than a blood-brother" – and in the whole of my being something began to settle and ease. Faint stirrings of overwhelming joy were filling my chest:

"In my humble opinion, you should make some kind of public statement and let the world breathe a momentary sigh of relief."

"That's exactly what I intend to do. Call a press conference and bring it all out into the open, before the eyes of the world. Only then, will I know peace," Amin declared and I believed him. He sensed this and hurried to confirm it: "You believe me!"

"With absolute belief," I did not hesitate to corroborate his words. "But..." I said.

"No 'buts'," he stepped in quickly to stop me.

"I mean, how will your controllers take this?"

"I have no controllers. I am the controller, the planner and the executor... and you have to understand, the ones who provide the financing for my activities don't belong to some kind of highly intellectual coterie, they have money and that's all."

"How can you explain this to them?" I insisted.

"In the language they understand, which is ultimately, at the end of the day, my own language."

"And the 'Jihad'?" I asked a pertinent question.

"Will find its rightful place."

"Which is?" I pressed him.

"The personal struggle of every man against his negative instinct," and he saw fit to add, "as you know as well as anyone."

He fell silent.

"May God go with you," I blessed him.

"And with you!" he responded at once, the response of a brother in faith to a brother in faith.

"The finger of God is everywhere," he continued with the fervour that had not yet abated, "I was hugely relieved when I heard they hadn't harmed you."

He finished his first cup of tea, and I poured him a second.

Amin switched from coffee to tea, perhaps to show solidarity with me, perhaps on account of some strange quirk of taste that he had developed among the Germans.

"In conclusion," my host declared, "you must go home and attend to whatever needs attending to in the village of Hasda. Reassure your patrons that a public statement is on its way. And I know you believe me, and you can convince your patrons and perhaps, by God's grace, we can open up the way, however narrow it may be, towards the salvation of our peoples and all peoples on the face of the earth."

"With God" was my benediction.

Amin sensed the potent hope in my words, and echoed them in Arabic: "*Allah maak!*"

I rose from my armchair. Amin accompanied me to the door, and I held out my hand. He shook it in all sincerity, and suddenly I felt his bony arms wrapped around me and found myself hugging the muscular, energetic frame of the man, so typically Bedou.

"I reserve this kind of embrace for a faithful brother," he intoned in my ear.

"Me too," I responded.

"Just one thing," I felt I had to stress, "take care of yourself! In a place where suicide-bombers exist, people don't delve deep into things, don't look at events in a spirit of wisdom and truth. Your activities are liable to arouse a willingness to murder the 'traitor' without examining your motives, without seeing the light generated by your words and your conduct."

"I can tell that your concern is sincere, but it is unnecessary. You forget that these are my brothers and compatriots, their thoughts are my thoughts, their way is my way, their perception my perception. Their instinctive penchant for murder and destruction is my instinctive penchant too."

"In other words," I tried to sum up, "the affiliation between you is strong, and the understanding even more so."

"Nicely put!" he declared.

"All the same, if you ever need a refuge, remember me."

"My refuge is my God, my strength – my brothers and compatriots. I thank you for your genuine offer, and you should understand, if I need a refuge and choose to come to you, I shall indeed be reckoned a traitor, with no excuses to offer for my actions and my treachery. In any case, the ways of God are hidden! Thank you. And now, to work!"

"To work!" I replied like an echo and there was another firm and sincere handshake, followed by an embrace no less firm and sincere. And hope soaring to the skies. We parted.

I went up to see Erika, who was burning up with curiosity.

"Well?" she asked, and then placing a silencing finger against my lips she went on to say: "Let me guess – world peace has been achieved! No more terror, no more innocent victims, an end to despair!"

"It seems to me you're a true poetess!"

"What does true poetess mean?"

"A true poet is a prophet."

"What have I prophesied?" she persisted.

"Just now, the coming of peace. Before that, the logical and final self-elimination of the white race."

"What makes you see these as prophecies?"

"Wishful thinking," I admitted shamefacedly.

"You're the real poet round here, not me."

"If you prefer," I conceded.

"And if your wife leaves you, come to me and don't worry, I am capable of being faithful."

"What has faithful to do with anything?" I retorted.

"I know the possessive types of the Middle East. I'll be a model wife to you, your durable property. Do with it as you please and if you get bored with it, sell it off cut-price. In other words: you won't find me an easy one to brush off. My love to your wife, and don't make any scenes. From a financial perspective you'll get my flat, which is worth half a million dollars. At least."

"It's obvious to me, the inverted age is taking you back to the era of servitude," I said, adding by way of elucidation: "Everything's based on money and everything is for sale."

"That's the way things are," she declared.

"I don't accept them," I retorted.

"You don't belong to the inverted age."

"Thank God for that!"

"Convey my offer to your wife."

"I'll do no such thing."

"Why is that?"

"It would hurt her."

"Your innocence makes me cringe! Tell her about my offer."

"I'm not interested."

"Not interested in what?"

"In passing on your offer. I'm not interested in you. I'm loyal to my wife. She's the one I want and she's the one I'm staying with."

"Those are the crazy genes of the Middle East. Anyway, give my love to your wife. She has a stubborn old mule for a husband. Tell her that. And tell her I admire her patience too."

"Now that's a message I might just pass on."

We parted. Parted for good.

I flew back to Israel. I invited the stewardesses to drink champagne with me to toast my successful endeavours and the fulfilment of my mission. Without asking what endeavours and what mission I was talking about – they took their glasses, clinked them and drank a toast to the success of Mister.... they mentioned my name. Without mispronouncing it.

CHAPTER TWENTY-ONE

Shmulik was waiting for me. He saw me from a distance, joined me and took my case and we went in together, into the VIP lounge again.

"One more trip like this and I'll be thinking I really am a VIP," was my jocular comment.

"You can think that way from this moment to the end of your time on the earth. In brief," he pressed me, "what is the outcome?"

"By the grace of God, we have averted evil and given good an opportunity to flourish..."

"What's all that supposed to mean?" – Shmulik demanded to know.

"From tomorrow," I began, getting down to the specifics, "we'll start the job of decontaminating the village of Hasda. We'll need to involve the Department of Health and in particular the national veterinary authority. I hope there is such a thing."

"If there isn't, we'll set it up this afternoon.

Put simply – what will these people be doing?"

"Putting an end to the disease, and the conditions it flourishes in."

He gave me a penetrating look, without a hint of sympathy, let alone consideration, even consideration of a direct and simple kind for someone who had been jetting around from here to there and back again, and getting a rather nasty job done in the process. He insisted on accompanying me to my home, where my wife was expecting me.

She had prepared my favourite meal, which wasn't exactly to Shmulik's taste – he being a native of the country with Ashkenazi roots.

All the same, he sat down and ate, constantly plying my wife with the kind of compliments she wasn't accustomed to, though no one could have been more deserving of them.

"And now, my trusty friend," Shmulik said, turning his full attention to me, "I'm looking for a plan of action. No artistic flourishes, just something realistic, carefully planned and properly executed."

I thought about this for a couple of minutes and then began dictating, while Shmulik took notes.

"Number one: all Jews to be evacuated from the village of Hasda, and Arab patients to be treated.

Number two: with the consent and active

assistance of the veterinary authority, all dogs in the village to be destroyed, irrespective of ownership, in fact – destroyed and incinerated. The houses in which the victims lived are also to be burned down to the ground.

Number three: not to give up on the idea of communal living. It may be that the Arabs will begin to appreciate it.

Number four: to monitor the media. A surprise announcement is expected from Doctor Amin Abu Halil, to which I must respond immediately."

A few days later the media, in all its various manifestations and in all corners of the world, reverberated to the shock reports of a press conference hosted by Dr Amin Abu Halil in the reception room of the German Prime Minister's residence, in which he admitted his blindness and quoted from the Koran – verse 224 of the Sura of the Cow – "And you shall pursue peace among mankind", and called the Arabs "errant brothers", turning light into darkness and darkness into light. And if they were to receive their just deserts, for the grief and misery they have unleashed, over a whole decade, upon their imaginary enemies and especially upon their own people, sending their precious and beloved children be suicide-bombers and destroy people like themselves – then all the chambers of Hell would be filled to overflowing, for centuries to come. And he is calling upon them with all his heart, to return to the bosom of true religion and uphold the commandment "to pursue peace among mankind" according to the spirit and the letter, seeing himself as the greatest sinner of them all, who at the instigation of Satan, tried to annihilate the holy people of God, from among whom came all the prophets, Moses and Jeremiah and Isaiah and the others, and all the illustrious kings of antiquity, Dawud the Great and Suleiman the wisest of men, of whom Islam speaks with awe and reverence. And now he feels it is the tongue of the Prophet with which he speaks, addressing his brothers and urging them to repent and adopt the injunction to pursue peace among mankind and inscribe it on their banners and flags and houses, and become the builders of a new world, where the sole king of every people, race and nation is the one God, the mighty and the merciful.

"On a personal basis I turn to my fellow student and fellow thinker," – and here he mentioned my name – "and I seek his pardon and forgiveness for all the evil that I have done to him and to his people, and here I swear before all the world that such a thing will never be repeated and my oath is sacred before God and man."

Shmulik came storming into my house

uninvited, waving the paper in which all Amin's astonishing statements were printed, hot off the press.

"You have to reply to it and at once!" he demanded. "Sit down and write and I'll take it to the relevant authorities. It seems everything that has happened has been for the best, as you write in your books. I'll sit and wait. I'd love a cup of coffee without sugar," he added, turning to my wife, who hurried away to borrow coffee from a neighbour.

"My brother in faith, in spirit and in origin, Dr Amin Abu Halil, your words presage what mankind has always dreamed of – an end to hatred and the shedding of blood – they will open up the gates of great love, lighting up for all mankind the abode of God, who is all-conquering love. Forgiveness is given you in full, not only because you are my brother, but also and especially, because there is nothing to forgive. And here is the place to ask you for pardon. 'If God Is for us, who can be against us?'" – I quoted.

Shmulik took the letter without reading it and hurried on his way. The letter was published in the papers, and read out on radio stations, Israeli and foreign, aired on TV channels, including, significantly, the Arabic ones, in tandem with the remarks of Dr Amin Abu Halil, my longstanding friend.

A few months later I received an official invitation to join the staff of the Muahadah Hakikiya – i.e. Covenant of Truth – medical centre, and the invitation was signed by the director-general of the centre, Professor Amin Abu Halil. I was sorry that my reply had to be negative, but the ways of medicine and science were no longer for me. Anyway, with all my heart I wished him every success in his important work, work vital for the peace and well-being of the world.

The reply was another invitation, in which the message was: To my elder brother, greetings! I understand your feelings, but if ever the idea appeals to you, you will be warmly welcomed in Riyadh. Keep to your new line of work, which is no less important than medicine and may even be a great deal more important.

Be strong and be bold.

He concluded his letter with the exhortation of the Biblical Joshua.

EPILOGUE

I met with Shmulik in the same café, at the same hour of the day, over the same unappetising liquid, which has to be paid for to be experienced. In his customary manner, Shmulik let the cat out of the bag straightaway:

"Jerusalem University wants you to lecture to the professors and all the academic staff in the faculty of medicine and life sciences, on recent events, from a purely medical perspective. They are thirsty for first hand knowledge and it seems to me they can't be denied it."

"They'll get comprehensive information, sure enough."

"Which days and hours are convenient for you?"

"They'll get comprehensive, exhaustive information in written form."

"You're going to write a book!"

"Yes."

"Why a book for Heaven's sake?" Shmulik persisted.

"As a native of this country, you know the stock answer to your question."

He smiled his broad and most radiant smile and at once rejoined: "Why not?"

We both laughed. A light and liberating laugh, composed of everything but tension and pressure, and needless to say, hatred directed at any person.

"Blessed be He who gave us life and existence and the opportunity to laugh" – Shmulik pronounced this benediction in all seriousness.

"One of your forbears was a rabbi!" I guessed.

"More than one."

"Why didn't you become a rabbi?"

He smiled thinly:

"So I'd have the privilege of facing your learned questions," – he suggested, not wanting to give offence.

"You've earned that."

"And now, in all seriousness, what answer should I give to those who sent me?"

"A detailed book is to be published soon, with a western-philosophical edge to it, and cutting no corners on the minutiae of the purely medical side of things, which is what they are interested in."

"When did you decide to write a book?"

"That's an interesting question, and it deserves a no less intriguing answer, even though it's all true... A few weeks ago," I continued, "I had the idea of changing my way of life. True, the alternative exists, but it costs a lot of money."

"How much, for example?" he interjected.

"More than a quarter of a million dollars. I discussed it with my wife and the idea appeals to her very much. In this case the question remains, how to earn a quarter of a million dollars honestly and honourably.

"The answer is," I continued, "to do what you're good at. Work at the job in which you've proved yourself. What I know how to do – is write. Our story began with a storm and it's ending with hope, you could call it a 'thriller' – a suspense novel, which the market is always thirsty for and prepared to pay for, assuming of course that the book is written with skill, is amusing, entertaining, has a lesson to teach, and even more important, brings hope and does not leave the reader feeling cheated. That's why I've decided to sit down and do this, in fact, to continue doing this, as the writing of the book has already started. I hope that before long it will be finished, and all the professors in Jerusalem, and not only there and not only professors, will hopefully be satisfied with the book and learn something from it."

"I'm sure I'll feature in the book," Shmulik

smiled a wry smile – "as one of the active participants, under a pseudonym of course."

"You certainly will be there – with your name in full."

"I'm not sure that's legal," he retorted, with a stern look on his face.

"We'll find out when the book's been published."

"Then it will be too late," Shmulik protested.

"So be it."

We shook hands, and parted company.

APPENDIX A

The Swiss, like other Europeans, up to their necks in affluence, are trying if not to depart from, at least to limit self-deception in all things relating to religion. The Swiss, like other Europeans, are steeped in the awareness that Christianity is not their religion. And all the churches that have been built, and the services that have been held there for a thousand years, and the colourful ceremonial, are not for them. "They are Jewish", weird and alien to the national spirit, and for this reason arousing natural opposition. Like their European brothers, the Swiss are seeking out a new god for themselves, or rather a new idol. And sure enough a new idol has presented itself to them, in the form of Buddhism. The Swiss are exceptional here too, and what appeals to them is surely some parallel between their land – high mountains, perpetual snow – and the essence of

Tibet, and the idol of the Tibetans, who wondrous to relate, is living and extant in the flesh, exiled from his homeland, and similar in many ways to that false god who laid upon them a yoke not to their liking – the new and exclusive idol of the Swiss is none other than the Dalai Lama, who during the time of our stay in Zurich came to visit the place and was greeted with restrained enthusiasm bordering on euphoria, authentically Swiss enthusiasm, and in authentically Swiss fashion – the restaurant in which His Holiness the Dalai Lama deigned to eat his lunch advertised the event prominently in the media, and opened up a waiting-list for applicants wishing to dine at the same time and in the same place, in his divine proximity, in exchange for a respectable fee.

The Swiss, like other Europeans, are entranced by nothingness and the void, although they call these things by all kinds of palliative names... there is no religion and no faith in Europe, and in Switzerland all the more so.

We felt no compulsion to dine in that restaurant, honoured as it was by the holy presence of the representative of nothingness and the void, and instead we watched the incessant stream of devotees, emanating from all corners of Europe and converging on Zurich, heading in the direction of the favoured restaurant. The devotees wore gowns of red and yellow, representing Tibetan Buddhism. Prominent among them was a large number of women, and among the women were many of middle age and above, and it is not in the nature of the neutral gown to accentuate or to hide any physical charms. Some of the gowns were open, and looked just like the kind of gowns that have a functional use in the bathroom.

In the streets of Zurich there were gigantic posters of the Dalai Lama with his humble and innocent smile. The current Dalai Lama does not insist on a sacred dimension or on enlightenment, but on his status as a Tibetan Buddhist from birth.

The Swiss are proud of their long-stemmed horns, virtually identical to the Tibetan Rag-Dung, which settles the argument over the origin of the Swiss. Of course, this is the opinion of the gown-wearers, male as well as female. I did not hear any other opinion expressed, despite the deafening peals of bells on Saturday evening and Sunday morning.

The visit of the exiled Dalai Lama to Zurich passed off quietly. What the future holds for the exiled Dalai Lama and for his European acolytes – is not easily foretold. Anyway, there was a flood of visitors to Zurich from states neighbouring Switzerland, not to mention neighbouring cantons, especially the German-speaking ones. On Buddhism in general and on the Dalai Lama in particular, I have written extensively in my previous books. In a nutshell, as I put it – Buddhism is nothing other than comprehensive suicide, of the body, the spirit and the soul. Recently, a fervent Buddhist responded with the claim that those who believe in God and turn to Him are nothing other than despicable cowards, from which it follows – he who spurns and dispels God is the fearless and heroic one, and not the reverse. Without wishing to stir up the sticky morass of claim and counter-claim too energetically, the kind of stirring that invariably and inevitably results in something very malodorous, it could be said, in writing of course and without entering into argument, of which Lao Tsze declares: "Arguing is not high-minded, and the high-minded do not argue" (Tao Teh Ching) – that I prefer to remain on the high-minded plane, as Lao Tsze has helpfully defined it.

Anyway, the Swiss authorities applauded the visit of the Dalai Lama to Zurich, which gave an added impetus to tourism, external and internal, an important and profitable sector of the Swiss economy, supplemented this time by the manufacture of gowns, Tibetan style, also useful in the bathroom and turning a handsome profit when sold at the same price to all (merely conjecture).

APPENDIX B

Every year, Zurich is decorated by puppets illustrating a certain theme. Two years ago these were colourful benches, this year bears appeared. King bears, bears in the costumes fashionable at the court of Louis XIV, astronaut bears, mountaineering bears, police bears, construction-worker bears, chocolate bears, etc. etc. Dolls, drawing the attention of tourists, clicking away with their cameras, especially tourists from the Far East, and providing national entertainment, uniquely Swiss, for the Swiss residents of the place.

In a central location, in a corner of the Bahnhoff, opposite the central railway station, stands a gigantic caricature of Einstein, dressed as a bear, and beneath it the caption: "Monsieur Al-Bear Einstein".

It is painful to see an eminent scientist, one of the greatest thinkers of the Twentieth Century, reduced to a laughing-stock for the benefit of yokels.

In my native country, the national poet, Yaborov, wrote a poem in praise of the Armenians. The emotional Armenians asked for and received from their government, permission to erect a memorial statue to Yaborov. At the base of the statue was the inscription: "To Yaborov, from the grateful Armenians."

Einstein, who carried the name of Switzerland from one end of the world to the other, was proud of his studies in Zurich and never had anything but good to say about Switzerland. And now, when everything has gone sour and Einstein is dead and buried, the manufacturers of chocolate and cuckoo-clocks are trying to give him the customary make-over.

The Swiss are in favour of integration and prepared to engage in incisive debate with all who oppose it, in any way. But, like other members of the family of German-speaking nations, they feel their skin crawling whenever conversation turns to that Jew who was indeed proud of his Swiss nationality – and yet this pride was not enough to turn him into a Swiss in their eyes.

Author's biography

Shlomo Kalo (1928-2014) was born in in Sofia, Bulgaria and was active in the anti-Fascist underground from the age of 12. At the age of 15, he was arrested and sent to a concentration camp. At the age of 18, he won a prize in a poetry competition. He Studied medicine in Prague where he also worked as a journalist. As an overseas volunteer for the newly established Israel, he was sent to train as a pilot in Olomouc and in 1949 immigrated to Israel. He was awarded M.Sc. in microbiology by the Tel-Aviv Univ. and Became director of medical laboratories in Israel's largest health care service.

The sharp turn in his life which occurred in the first week of 1969 has been reflected ever since in his creation. 80 titles of his were published in Israel: fiction and literary non-fiction written in a variety of genres. His works have so far been translated and published in 17 countries.

Kalo was nominated for the receiving of the Nobel Prize between the years 2008-2014.

Some fiction titles written by Shlomo Kalo's that are available on Amazon:

THE CHOSEN An Epic Novel based on the Biblical Story of Daniel, in one volume or in three:

Book I: THE YOUTH
Book II: THE PROPHET
Book III: A MAN MUCH LOVED
LILI A novel of Love Suspense and Redemption of the true kind
ATHAR a Holocaust Memoir
FOREVERMORE Gripping documented stories from Jewish history
ERRAL An autobiographical novel
THE   TROUSERS – Parables for the 21st Century